PAN

Half English, half Tibetan, Chhimi Tendur-La grew up in Hong Kong, London, New Delhi and Colombo. He now lives in Colombo with his wife Samantha and his daughter Tara. He has written plays and fiction for local publications. His first book, *The Amazing Racist*, was published in 2015.

PANTHER

PANTHER

CHHIMI TENDUF-LA

HARPER

First published in India in 2015 by Harper
An imprint of HarperCollins *Publishers*

P-ISBN: 978-93-5177-220-0
E-ISBN: 978-93-5177-221-7

2 4 6 8 10 9 7 5 3 1

HarperCollins *Publishers*
A-75, Sector 57, Noida, Uttar Pradesh 201301, India
1 London Bridge Street, London, SE1 9GF, United Kingdom
Hazelton Lanes, 55 Avenue Road, Suite 2900, Toronto, Ontario M5R 3L2
and 1995 Markham Road, Scarborough, Ontario M1B 5M8, Canada
25 Ryde Road, Pymble, Sydney, NSW 2073, Australia
195 Broadway, New York, NY 10007, USA

Typeset in 11/14.5 Sabon by
R. Ajith Kumar

Printed and bound at
Thomson Press (India) Ltd

*To Liz the Fizz,
my incredible mother.*

AUTHOR'S NOTE

Neither the school nor the miscreant students in this novel represent, in any way, the calibre of education in Sri Lanka. In my own experience, students here are right up there with the most disciplined, respectful, lawful and intelligent in the world.

Similarly, the depiction of the war in this book is fictitious and I have taken the liberty of inventing a terrorist organization so as to make it clear that I do not pretend to have firsthand knowledge or experience of the actual war, the trauma of which is beyond my understanding.

There are some bad people in this book. Very bad. This is fiction.

In reality, Sri Lanka is the friendliest and most beautiful country I have ever been to, where the people are warm and generous hosts who love a good laugh. It is a country so rich with culture and heritage that it would need a book far longer and better written than this one to do it justice.

If you have never been before, it's time to visit.

ONE

I see you.

What are you, like twelve or thirteen? Legs like toothpicks, body and face all ribs and cheekbones.

And that hair. Come on, what is it? Like the friggin' barbed wire at the Panthers' camp.

I see you with a hand-me-down cracked bat, creaming a leather ball in a sock hanging from the branch of a mango tree.

I see Appa grinning. Proud of you, because there's nothing that means more to him than family.

Nothing that means more to him than his boy.

So you follow him everywhere. Follow him to work in his van. Follow him to meet his friends. Even follow him, sometimes, without his knowing.

Like now, when he looks left, looks right, before darting into a roofless cinema house. You crouch, run closer to a tree by the window. Like a commando. Like a Panther.

He takes his shirt off.

He what? You rub your eyes.

1

He's in the arms of a lady. Younger, fairer, smoother than Amma. She cups his rice-belly in her hands as he closes the curtains.

You throw up. Throw up the lunch Amma made. Appa's favourite food. The food he's using as fuel to be with another lady.

The next day, a trishaw stops outside your collapsed front wall. Appa shouts at you, 'Get in the friggin' tree.'

Your arms extend out. 'Why, Ap–'

'Now.'

Three men squeeze out of the back of the trishaw, each dude's machine gun clinking off the next's. They wear mismatched camouflage combat gear and square-peaked caps.

The driver of the trishaw's in sarong, vest and beret. You know this crazy cookie. He's the dude who speaks in riddles, uses his hands a lot, smokes, grumbles, strokes his pointed goatee beard. Everyone thinks he's a genius, but Appa says he's just a film critic in a town where films aren't made because of the war.

'How, how, how?' Appa grovels towards them. Bent at the waist, small steps, dragging feet, hands up in prayer.

The first of the men swipes off his hat, looks up, blinks, challenges the glare of the sun. You've never seen such white eyes before. Such black skin before. So black you can't tell if the dude has a moustache.

Down on his knees, Appa grabs at each of the men's thighs. Crying like a little bitch. Embarrassing you.

The second dude takes off his cap. Looks up the mango

tree. Looks up at you. Points. Turns to speak to Appa.

Back on his feet, Appa scampers to get between the second man and you. 'Please, please, please.' He turns to you. 'Go higher, higher.'

The other men laugh.

They stand in a semicircle. Appa between them. Like he's an actor performing a tragedy. The film critic is unimpressed by his performance. So unimpressed he punches Appa in the stomach. Elbows him in the face. Spits at his feet.

And your father is now in his jungies. His undies. Dancing. Hands in the air, feet up and down. His tears hitting the friggin' red clay of your garden until the men lower their guns and stop laughing. Until the film critic leaves.

While Appa pulls up his trousers, the men point up to you again. Appa pushes at their chests. Lifts his palms up, shouts, 'Wait.'

He runs into the house through the gap where the door used to be. Comes back out, Amma crying behind him, with her gold chain. Her gold headdress, her rings. Her wedding jewellery.

Then, just like that, the men are gone.

You wake up the next morning to Amma's crying. 'Appa's left me. Appa's left me.'

'All men are pig assholes,' Akka says. 'Typical. Pig. Bloody. Asshole.'

At first you want to defend Appa. Then you realize he's not abandoned just Amma and Akka, he's abandoned you. And you were meant to be his pride and friggin' joy.

You break down. Throw fists at trees, kick at chickens. You burn presents from him. Tear up photographs of him. Toss his junk on a fire.

A war zone is a breeding ground for gossip. Gossip breeding like dengue mosquitoes at building sites in towns where things are built, not blown up.

This is what people say.

Appa is no terrorist, but you knew that, no?

He's neither a Tiger nor a Panther. Not fighting for a Tamil homeland. For Eelam. Couldn't give a shit. Couldn't give a fat shit, they say.

Hates fights. Just loves love. Loves women. Loves your amma. Taking her faults in his stride.

Now the gossips change *loves* to *loved*.

They say your appa was always telling your amma things. Things like, 'There is great value in shaving one's legs if one's legs are female.'

This much is true. You've heard that. Most nights. Most mornings. Sometimes over lunch or with a cup of tea. Sometimes while in the car.

Amma never listened but Appa let it go. No complaints. Hell, one physical fault was nothing to worry about for a man as chilled as your appa.

Things, they say, started to go wrong when your amma found a waffle iron in a bombed-out restaurant.

You had no electricity, so Appa tapped into the local army camp's generator. A military policeman caught him. Appa bribed him. With waffles.

But he was running short of ingredients, so he used his van to spy for the army. They paid him in flour, jaggery, eggs and milk.

The gossips say Amma fell in love with waffles. Thought of waffles first thing in the morning. Dreamt of waffles at night. With this obsession came rapid weight gain.

And once your amma hit one hundred kilos, your appa could no longer ignore her body hair, so they say.

Appa, like most men in these parts, had needs, and if people in these parts had needs, they visited the hairless wife of the unemployed film critic.

They say it started off as business only. But now they think it's love. They assume Appa ran off with her and this assumption looks strong. She's vanished too.

The unemployed film critic, a man of honour in his own eyes, offers to keep Amma in the manner to which she has grown accustomed; but without his wife's body, he has no income.

You've no father. No need for a damn stepfather, you tell Amma. But your family needs an income. So Amma responds to a cold call asking Tamils to serve the community. You cats are accepted into the programme. Woohoo. High five. Hugs and kisses. Finally, maybe, some food.

But. Oh shit.

You've been duped into acting as human shields at a Panther base.

The Panthers? They're a breakaway group of separatists fighting for their own land.

The Panther base is an old school, the classrooms made of balanced corrugated iron sheets. You're tasked with cleaning out guns in Grade Three, Amma and Akka stitching up the holes in old uniforms in Grade Six.

In the distance, there is a splattering of gunfire, the odd explosion, but for the most part things are silent. Until a chopper flies over the base, guns at the ready. The Panther hierarchy leg it into an underground bunker. Their footsoldiers marshal the rest of you in the assembly hall, a solid concrete structure, at the front of which is a Hindu shrine; next to that, a cross.

'Let them hit us here,' a Panther says. 'Strike our women and children. Strike our gods and then we'll see.'

The bullets pepper the roof like monsoon rain. Digging holes in the cobbled floor. You bury your head between your knees but can still hear the chopper double back. But it doesn't fire this time, wary of the wrath of the gods, perhaps. Wary of hurting kids.

Calm. You breathe in again. The chopper's gone.

You hug Amma, your left hand stuck in the flaps of her belly. Silence … As if you're wearing earplugs.

You watch Akka as she looks down at her arm. Holds it. Blood squeezing through her fingers.

She screams the friggin' joint down.

Amma pushes you away, howls. 'Why, why, why? Why Akka? Why us?' Throws her weight at Akka. 'This is all Appa's fault.'

The Panthers are no pussycats, but neither are they completely heartless. They have a rule that if a child is hurt in any attack, one parent can take that child to a doctor. Akka, older than you by two years, is still a child. Still qualifies.

You help Akka to the door, her legs dragging behind her for no reason, since she was shot in the arm. You come back for Amma, who is face-down on the floor. Still asking questions.

Then the doors open. Akka goes first, then Amma. But you're held back.

'Only one child,' they say. 'One child and a parent.'

'But—'

'That's the way it is,' they say.

Leaving Akka in the arms of a female Panther, Amma comes back in. Tears battling over her fat cheeks. 'I love you, my boy.' She squashes the breath out of you. 'More than anything.'

She turns to leave, but you tug at her arm. 'Amma, don't leave me.'

'It's just for an hour or two.'

The door closes. Locks.

You don't know why, but you have a feeling you'll never see her again. Never see Appa, never see Akka again.

Now I see you sitting in the corner of Grade Three, knees drawn to your chest.

You've never been in a sauna, I know that, but this is what it's like. The sun heats up the tin roof above you, so you sweat till your muddy t-shirt is drenched, but still your teeth chatter. You shiver. It's fear, it's sadness, it's anger.

You're helpless.

You want to cry. Want to shout out for Amma and

Akka. Want to curse Appa. But you know you'll never see them again. You know this because standing over you is Tarzan Subramanium.

Tarzan is topless, muscles rippling, moustache twitching. He looks happy and sad at the same time. Angry and chilled. His eyes smile but his mouth frowns. That's some skill, you think.

And this man, Tarzan, he's telling you bad things about your mother. That your mother jumped ship. Took her daughter south. Sacrificed one child to save another. 'That shit ain't fair,' he says.

'But, but …'

'What happens to you?' he asks.

'What happens to me?'

'You become an orphan. No one to care for you. No one to hug.'

'Can I come with you?'

'Little man, I have work to do.' He lifts you to your feet. Pats your back. Raises the stub of his index finger to your tears. 'Causes to defend. But I promise I'll come check on you when I'm back. Promise I'll look out for you. Anything else I can do?'

'Find my appa. My amma. My akka.'

'They're gone, kid.' He claps his hands. 'Like that. Gone. You have to accept that, little man.'

And before you can ask him anything more, Tarzan has gone too.

Your mouth opens to scream but nothing comes out. You just have to accept that you're a bastard now.

Have to accept that I can't see you any more.

TWO

Prabu crouched on the cricket pitch, wearing cricket whites, his top button fastened, collar up. The waist of his trousers balanced on his nipples. If he'd had a wallet in the rear pocket of his pants, he would have had to reach over his shoulder to fetch it.

But he had no money. Not even a one-cent coin. So he had no use for a wallet.

If he had money, maybe he'd have used fairness creams for his black skin. That's the shit in South Asia, no? So if he had money, what would he buy? Fair and Handsome? Fair and Lovely? Fair and Over There? Fair and Nice Pair?

Maybe if he had money, he'd have parents. Maybe they'd have told him to leave more space between his ears and the top of his trousers. *And* they'd sure as shit have told him not to speak to a cockroach in public.

The cockroach looked out of place on the cricket pitch. On its back, motionless, twig legs pointed up like pupils' hands in a class where everyone knew everything.

Squatting, his backside millimetres from the red clay

wicket, Prabu flicked the cockroach over with the tips of his fingernails.

It didn't move.

Prabu looked to the skies, searching for any god willing to help. But gods always demanded something in return, and what did Prabu have to sacrifice. But for the damn cockroach.

He blinked. In that moment, the cockroach's antennae straightened, wings flapped, legs heaved like the oars of a rowing crew. Star-jumping back on to his feet, Prabu guided the cockroach to freedom, his shadow looming over it like the 2004 tsunami.

To his left, the scoreboard hung off a rusty double-decker London bus. Next to that, rolled clay under a corrugated iron sheet. They called it the pavilion. From there, Coach Silva wobbled towards Prabu. Rubbed his rice-belly, stretched his two chins into one. 'Black boy, get off the bloody wicket.'

Prabu recognized the name on the back of the man's shirt. 'Please, Coach, I just make sure cockroach is safe.'

Coach Silva's crooked smile showcased a set of teeth made crimson by the betel leaf he chewed. He pointed at the cockroach. 'That one?'

Prabu's chickpea-head rolled around in a figure of eight. 'Yes, sir.'

'Poor little bugger.' Coach Silva leaned over it. 'Looks so lost out here. Nice of you to want to help it.'

'He reminds me of a cockroach I knew.'

Coach Silva chuckled. Spat out red juice that looked like blood. 'Poor bugger probably didn't see that sign.

The one that says stay off the wicket. Even if it did, cockroaches can't read, no?'

Easy question, even for Prabu. 'No, sir.'

'Probably didn't even see the rope cordoning off the wicket. Must have just slipped under it.'

Prabu giggled. *Sweet little innocent cockroach.*

'So it was a wasted journey for me, really.' Coach Silva lifted his hand up. 'Was chilled in the pavilion. Under the fan and out of the hot bloody sun. Only came out here 'cause I thought someone'd ignored my sign. Ignored my barriers. My wishes.' He mocked a laugh. 'But now I realize the poor bloody cockroach can't read.'

Prabu bowed. 'Correct, sir.'

'Will just head back to the pavilion then.' He curled one of the four hairs on his head around his finger. 'Oh wait, one thing, boy.'

'Yes, sir.'

'Can you read?'

Prabu straightened his back. Hand on chest. 'Very well, sir.'

'Clever boy.' Coach Silva pinched both of Prabu's cheeks. 'Maybe you couldn't read this sign? Can't read English?'

'Can read, sir. But the cockroach looked like it is about to become dead and thusfore I decide to make help.'

Coach Silva lifted a hand behind his right ear. The ear like trampled cabbage. Had more hair on it than his head did. 'Sorry, don't think I heard you right. So you did read the sign?'

Prabu's neck locked. 'Maybe, sir, I—'

'You did or you didn't, boy.'

'Sir, but the cockroach needed—'

'This cockroach?' Coach Silva raised his foot above it. Prabu closed his eyes. Dug his chin into his chest. What he heard could have been a papadum being bitten into. Could have been a leaf being crushed. But even a boy as backward as Prabu knew better.

Coach Silva had stamped the cockroach into a paste, looked like katta sambol. Lips puckered, he made a kissing noise. 'Shane Warne, come here.'

A spiky-furred dog shuffled towards him, head down, tail as stiff as a blocked hose. Coach Silva peeled a rubber slipper off his bloated foot. Rubbed the remnants of the dead cockroach on the dog's coat.

The dog, Shane Warne, snarled, backed into the gap between Prabu's legs.

'Who the hell are you?' Coach Silva asked.

Prabu pointed a finger at his own chest. 'You talk to me?'

Coach Silva sat on a plastic chair, the legs of which spread under his weight. 'No, I'm talking to the bloody dog.'

Looking down at the dog, Prabu wondered how it would respond.

Coach Silva hurled his slipper at Prabu's face. 'I'm talking to you, idiot retard. Kneel down in front of me.'

Prabu dug a cockroach's wing out of his moustache. Brushed clay off his elbows. On his knees, he turned to the row of palm trees on the boundary under which

Mr Carter smoked a rolled-up cigarette. 'Sir,' he called out. 'Carter sir, please help.'

Mr Carter glided over the sandy outfield, more like a beach than a lawn. His hair, the colour of a Buddhist monk's robes, pasted down with sweat. 'What's eating you, little man?' He strode past Prabu. Extended his hand out to Coach Silva. 'I wonder if you remember me.'

Coach Silva squeezed out of his chair. Grabbed Mr Carter's hand in both of his. 'Yes. Yes. Mr Carter, the Brit.'

'Australian, mate.'

'Ah.' Coach Silva adopted an accent more Chinese than Australian. 'Put another sheila on the barbie.'

'Shrimp,' Mr Carter said. 'Never mind. Look, we have to make a change to the playing eleven.'

'Too late, boss.' Coach Silva caught the breath he appeared to have lost when lifting his jumbo ass off the chair. 'Team sheet in the hands of the umpire already.'

'Look, simply no option.' Mr Carter shook his head, sprinkling sweat on Prabu. 'The team changes. This champ's a new player sent to us by the defence ministry. Freed from an IDP camp yesterday. Signed up by our school this morning.'

Coach Silva's nose pinched towards Prabu. 'This Tamil boy?'

'Hang on there, chief.' Mr Carter raised his palm. 'Have some respect. He's a flag bearer for internally displaced people being integrated back into society. Principal Uncle signed up for this.'

'Team sheet's in, tactics down,' Coach Silva said. 'Not a bugger's going to tell me to change the team.'

'BBC's on its way to film him for the news, shown around Asia. Around the world. The boy plays. Simple as.'

Placing the back of his hand against his forehead, Coach Silva rolled his neck. 'Once you give the team sheet to the umpire, that's it. They're not allowed to return it.'

'I've been in this country long enough to know that money talks many languages.' Mr Carter took out a thousand-rupee note. 'One of them is Sinhalese.'

'Normal times, I can make an umpire dance for a thousand. Not this one. Bugger's so honest, even turned down a bribe from the minister of bribery.'

'Ah jeez.' Mr Carter took his phone out. 'Hell can we do then?'

'Give him two thousand.'

'Done.' Mr Carter turned towards the umpire.

'No, no.' Coach Silva shook his fists. 'You mad? White bugger like you'll get charged five times the going rate.' He snatched the money out of Mr Carter's hand. 'The Tamil boy, what is his name?'

Prabu rose on to his tiptoes, his head level with Mr Carter's sweaty nipples. 'The Prabu.'

'How was it, boy?' Coach Silva asked. 'The camp?'

Prabu knew his lines. 'Very nice. Better than my house.'

'You were there since the war ended in September 2009?'

'Yes, sir.'

'But the war ended in May 2009.'

'Yes, sir.'

Facing Mr Carter, his eyelids drooping like sleeping

bats, Coach Silva said, 'Bugger's too spaced out for my team. Need to win this bloody game.'

'Look, he's no charity case, mate. Class act. Colonel Thisara told me he's good enough for the Sri Lanka Under-seventeens.'

'Colonel Thisara … I know that name.' Coach Silva cocked his head to one side. 'Commander of his camp?'

'Yep.' Carter handed him a file. 'Prabu's rules. Sign the card after each session.'

Prabu caught a whiff of something exotic that the other boys sprayed under their arms as they finished their warm-ups.

Back in the north, he'd only had talcum powder for sweat and even that only for special occasions like funerals – until there were too many of them.

The other boys dropped to their knees, one by one, bowed their heads and touched Coach Silva's bushy feet, took his blessing, sprinted back to the pavilion.

Prabu jogged after them.

He ambled into the men's room, standing outside two cubicles, both of which had doors. Behind them was a sink with running water, and to top it all off, on either side of the squatting pans, there were raised levels for his feet.

Lowering his trousers, he squatted so he could clutch his knees while he relieved himself. To save time, he had breakfast, dipping a toothpick into a bag of peppered pineapple slices.

'Ping pang pong, it stinks in here,' a boy said in refined

English. 'Wouldn't come in here, lads. Floating turds. All. Over. The. Place.'

The boy kicked open the door to Prabu's cubicle, forcing one of the hinges out of its slot. Prabu recognized him, didn't know how. Indika Jayanetti, the school's cricket captain. The superstar player.

'So sorry, machan.' Indika blew hair out of his face. 'Didn't know anyone was in there.'

Prabu finished what he was doing, rose to his feet, washed his backside from a burst tap. When he exited the cubicle, he found Indika balanced on one foot, peeing into the neighbouring squatting pan.

Mr Carter had already told Prabu off for staring too much, but now he couldn't help it. Indika had skin the colour of milk tea, a European nose, not just a pair of rocket-launching nostrils. Man, the dude shone like the girls in those fairness cream ads Appa used to watch with his hands in his pockets.

'What the hell are you staring at?' Indika asked.

'You have the white paint on your nose.' Prabu reached for Indika's face. 'Shall I wipe it off for you?'

'No, no. It's sunblock. So I don't get too black.' He looked Prabu up and down. 'Not that being black is bad.'

'I know.' Prabu tried to turn a tap on but it came loose in his hands.

'Read that, machan.' Indika pointed at a sign above the cracked mirror.

It said: 'By order of the sports ministry, vandals will be subject to prostitution.'

This was meant to be funny. Prabu could tell by the look on Indika's face.

Indika looked at the tap. 'Are you a vandal?'

'No, I'm a Tamil.' Prabu's gaze lost itself in Indika's hair, lighter both in shade and weight than his own. Certainly less greasy. 'Your name is called Indika Jayanetti?' Prabu raised his palms together, as if in prayer. 'Honour to meet you.'

Indika turned his lower body to face away from Prabu. 'Dude, keep your eyes above my waist.'

Prabu didn't understand that comment. He'd never looked below Indika's cushion lips. His slanted eyes. To overcompensate, he stared up at the ceiling, getting hit on the mouth by a drop of gooey liquid from the mildewed roof. 'I am your new opening batting partner. My name is called the Prabu Ramanathan.'

Coach Silva limped into the bathroom and slapped away Prabu's extended hand. 'Make yourself scarce,' he said to Indika.

Prabu flicked his tongue back and forth in the gap where his front tooth should have been.

'I read your rules,' Coach Silva said.

'Thank a lots.'

'When did you last attend school?'

Prabu rubbed his forehead. 'Sir, maybe I was eleven at that time.'

'Six years ago?'

Prabu counted on his hands without giving an answer.

'Take your time.' Coach Silva looked down at his Casio watch.

'Yes, what you said.'

'According to your rules, you have to pass the end-of-term exams in December for Grade Eleven. This is A Level studies.'

'Yes, they tell to me this.'

'Or your scholarship and sponsorship are removed, and you get sent back to the camp.'

Prabu nodded. 'Correct.'

'I have many players who've been at school all their lives. Fail those bloody exams.'

'I work hard, sir,' Prabu said. 'Very hard. Anything's possible.'

'Be a big change of life if you fail. From an elite school in Colombo's Cinnamon Gardens, back to an overcrowded camp?'

'I do everything not to fail, sir.'

'Guess you better.' Coach Silva held Prabu's shoulders. 'You said your IDP camp leader was Colonel Thisara.'

Prabu looked down at Coach Silva's feet. Knew what was coming. 'Yes, sir.'

'Colonel Thisara may be the officer in charge of a camp, but you and I both know it's not for IDPs. So tell me, boy, where the hell are you really from?'

THREE

I'm back and I can see you because the war's over.

You're in an army truck, hands held together on your lap as if they're cuffed. But they're not.

Finally, you're free, you think.

On either side of you, boys your age or younger, in clothes covered in dried mud. Opposite you, a girl, just twelve.

Each of you to be looked after in a camp because you have nowhere to go. No parents. No families.

Two army guards stand on the back step of the truck. There to protect you, you guess. There to protect your childhood.

The truck ascends a hill overlooking rubber estates and coconut plantations. The camp's surrounded by barbed wire, armed sentries in towers, but the dorm rooms you are led into are enclosed in glass.

You don't feel trapped any more.

'Children, we admire you.' You kids sit on a raised concrete ledge looking down at a man in civilian clothes.

He's bald, tall, broad-chested and always smiling. Next to him, a woman, almost the size of Amma, translates everything he says into Tamil. 'My name is Colonel Thisara and I have worked hard to earn my rank. But I'd like you beautiful children to call me Uncle Thisara.' He smiles. 'Can you all say Uncle Thisara?'

You whisper to yourself, 'Uncle Thisara.' No one else speaks.

'We'll give it time,' Colonel Thisara says. 'I have four children of my own, and I love kids. There's nothing better in the world than kids. My kids live in Colombo, go to school, have opportunities that you have not had because of war. The reason I am here is to give you opportunities. Because now I don't think I have four kids, I have fifty-eight kids. You are all my kids. Would you like that?'

Silence.

Colonel Thisara laughs. Taps the translator on the back. 'I'll take that as a yes. I admire you kids. We admire you kids. War is tough enough with the support of family, but you have survived it on your own. I tell this to my kids and they are amazed. They say they couldn't have coped, but you have, and now you're here. It's our job to make you feel welcome, loved. It's our job to help you overcome your memories, your fears, and it is our job, where possible, to reunite you with your families.'

Smiles break out on the faces of the other kids, but not yours. You won't allow yourself to have false hope.

'We want you to play without fear,' Colonel Thisara says. 'Love without fear. Learn without fear. The guards around the camp are here for you. So you feel safe.'

You look up at the towers, wondering why the guards are pointing their guns in and not out.

'I'm not going to lie to you,' Colonel Thisara says. 'They're also here to stop you from leaving, but that's just short term. It's our belief that you must stay here for a few months before you're ready for the outside world. More than that, we need to know where you are if we find any family of yours.'

A few of the other kids smile again. You look around the room. Some of the children next to you look to be sixteen, seventeen. Maybe eighteen. Others much younger.

Now the war is over, I wonder, who has more hope? The younger ones who have some of their childhood left? Or the older ones who can leave their childhoods behind?

'We'll show you to your beds now,' Colonel Thisara says. 'I think you'll find them comfortable, but I suggest you use the mosquito nets. Tomorrow, we will start teaching you skills that you can use when you leave us. Firstly, I must apologize, but we are short of a Tamil teacher, but maybe it's good that you learn Sinhala until we find one. Maybe learn some English too. You'll also have to eat our food, but it's spicy and it's rice, so you should like it.'

And you do. The first meal you have is like a race. The girl next to you funnels balls of rice and dhal into her mouth as if her hand is a spade. But you come up for breath first, your plate cleaned of all the vegetable curries.

'More.' Your first audible words at camp.

A lady in a sari says, 'Okay, but just this once. After today, we need to eat healthily.'

'More,' you say.

You're eating so much I know what's going to happen. After your next plate, before you can beg for another helping, your stomach rumbles.

'Toilet?' you ask. 'Toilet, toilet, toilet.'

The woman points you outside, but first you have to be cleared by a guard at the door.

'Toilet.'

The guard directs you to a hut made of corrugated iron sheets. You push the door so hard the whole structure shakes. You squat above a hole dug in the ground. 'Agh.'

It hurts. Crapping solids hurts.

You wake up in the dorm. Sweating. Wide-eyed. It's hard to sleep in this silence. The bed to your right is empty. The twelve-year-old mute is not around. Has he escaped? Why would he want to?

Running to the door, you look outside. A light shines on you from a guard tower. But there's no gunfire. No shelling.

The spotlight swings to shine on a tree and you follow its glare. The twelve-year-old mute is lying on a branch, his head resting on his hands, his eyes open.

Maybe he doesn't know how to sleep in a bed.

The girls gather outside for cooking classes. They begin to smile. The woman in the sari with her arm around them. Encouraging them.

You're inside. A man in blue overalls teaches you and your peers about plumbing. In the afternoon, they teach you electrical works. In the evening, the woman in the sari reads you passages from English books. Most of the other kids don't understand, but you do, you don't know how.

You're allowed to watch one hour of TV a night. Nothing showing fighting. Repeats of old comedies and cricket matches. Repeats of Sri Lanka winning the World Cup in 1996.

Colonel Thisara puts his arm around your shoulder. 'You play cricket?' he asks in English.

'I am love cricket,' you mumble.

Colonel Thisara pats your back, says something to the guards in Sinhala and leaves.

The next morning, a match is arranged. The army soldiers against the kids.

Throwing a bat to you, Colonel Thisara says, 'You open.' He turns to the lady in the sari. 'I have a feeling about this kid.'

The bowler passes his machine gun and helmet to the umpire, who has a machine gun of his own.

Rolling up his sleeves, he then tosses a brand new leather ball from hand to hand. Spitting on it. Rubbing it on his camouflage trousers.

He sprints in, leaps in the air, bangs the ball in short so it bounces up to your ears.

You bend backwards, at the waist, guiding the ball over the wicketkeeper's head, clearing the barbed wire.

Colonel Thisara laughs. 'Six.'

Every morning, before breakfast, everyone in the camp gathers to watch you bat. Your technique is perfect. You extend your right arm with a high elbow, play straight through the ball with no gap between bat and pad.

'I have a plan for you.' Colonel Thisara's smile is wider, whiter, more beautiful than ever. 'If you keep working hard, your English improves, and you continue to bat like God, I have a plan for you.'

FOUR

Learn Good Overseas School set an imposing total for Mother Nelson Mahatma International College to chase down. Prabu prepared to bat, the midmorning sun rising behind the bowler's parachute ears.

The first ball fizzed off the middle of the pitch, the sound reminding Prabu of a rocket being launched. He smelt leather, ducked too late. The ball whacked into his jaw like a boxer's uppercut. Knocked him off his feet, but he managed to pirouette away from the stumps.

Indika dashed to him, crouching and holding his head. 'Shit, are you okay, machan?'

Trying not to tremble, Prabu spat out blood. 'My head is paining.'

'You'd better retire hurt,' Indika said.

Prabu felt his chin. *This not paining. I am too much strong. This not paining.* 'No, No. I wait a long time for this. I not go.'

Oh, shit the panties, this is bloody paining.

He bent to face the next ball. Left-handed, Prabu brought the bat down from well above his head and,

25

using his rubber wrists, caressed the ball to the long-on boundary, forcing a murder of crows to take flight.

'Get this black bastard out,' the wicketkeeper said to the bowler. 'Must be a bloody terrorist, the bastard.'

Indika tapped the pitch with his bat as he walked up to Prabu. 'Ignore it. No imagination, these pricks.' He smiled at the wicketkeeper. 'Concentrate on the game, bro.'

'You want this?' The wicketkeeper grabbed his groin. Spat on the ground. 'You have fair skin because your father has money to pay Russian hookers.'

Indika took his helmet off and stuck out his chest. 'Your knob's so small, he can get you a discount.'

The wicketkeeper turned towards the pavilion. Clapped his hands above his head. Five men, in black trousers and Nehru-collared white shirts, moved towards the boundary.

'You know who my father is?' the wicketkeeper asked.

'No.' Indika moved closer. Jaw to jaw. 'Do you?'

The umpire, sweating in a long white lab coat, walked down the pitch. Put his arms over Indika's and Prabu's shoulders. Said to the wicketkeeper, 'Sorry, sir, I'll handle this.'

Out of earshot, Prabu asked, 'Who's his father?'

Looking around, the umpire formed a huddle with Indika and Prabu. 'Boy's name is Suresh. Father's the minister of glorious festivities. Uncle's the minister of fancy goods. Aunt is the minister of weddings. The men on the boundary are the boy's personal bodyguards. This guy's actually the sensible son. Brother goes by the name Shock Ice. Animal.'

Indika shut his eyes, nodded. 'Understood. I've got this.' He ambled back to Suresh, his palms facing out. 'I'm sorry, sir, I didn't realize whom I was talking to. I have enormous respect for your father, uncle and aunt.'

Suresh, wicketkeeping gloves still on, tapped Indika on the head. Signalled for him to go on batting.

Prabu felt something tickling inside him; a warm feeling he hadn't felt since his father praised him for cutting down coconuts. He thumped his chest. Stared down the wicket at Indika, his protector.

Prabu reminded himself to concentrate on the cricket. Everything flew off the middle of his bat, his bat like a wand blessed by a greater being.

The crowd called out his name.

Apu Apu Apu.

They got it wrong. Mr Carter stood in front of them. They stopped chanting for a few seconds before starting again.

Prabu Prabu Prabu.

He lost control of his smile. The last time a crowd had cheered him like this was when he beat Swift Feet Siva to the top of the camp tower.

With four runs needed for victory, Prabu danced down the pitch, lofted the ball straight into the crowd.

Indika kissed Prabu on the head, then spat, grimaced, wiped his lips, held his nose.

'You smell something funny?' Prabu asked.

'Nothing, machan.' Indika took his hand off his nose

to catch a towel chucked at him by a girl he didn't appear to know. 'What a bloody innings,' he said. 'You can't disguise it. You're Brian Lara.'

'No, no, I am not Brian Lara.' He tilted back his borrowed batting helmet. 'I am Prabu Ramanathan.'

Indika strutted off the pitch, his hand up to accept high fives. One of them from Coach Silva in front of a BBC camera.

'This is a future player for our country.' Coach Silva ruffled Prabu's hair. Tried to, at least, but it wouldn't budge. 'I do whatever I can to make him feel welcome, like one of us.'

'He is one of us, surely.' One man reached out his hand to Prabu. 'Well played, son. Astonishing innings.'

Prabu twitched his nose, looked up, one eye closed.

'Astonishing is a good thing,' the man said.

The BBC cameras roamed the grounds, taking background shots.

'Jayanetti, how you bugger?' Coach Silva hugged the man. 'You've put on.' Was he Indika's father?

'Too many reasons to eat, no?' Jayanetti said. 'You've gone down. Sick?'

Coach Silva shook his head fast enough to make his cheeks dance. Cupped Jayanetti's ear. 'You know that baby we adopted?'

'Kella from Negombo?'

'Cried for hours every night. I allowed my wife to take her to a doctor who wouldn't ask where the baby came from.'

'The adoption wasn't legal?'

'Depends who asks.'

'If the police ask?'

'I say legal. So the doctor told us that the baby was fine. Just a bloody crier.'

'So sorry to hear,' Jayanetti said. 'Must be exhausting.'

'No, no.' Coach Silva mimicked cradling a baby. 'The joys of children.'

Jayanetti smiled. 'Better now, then?'

'Don't know. Returned her a week ago.'

'Wait, wait, wait.' Jayanetti kid-punched Coach Silva's shoulder. 'You're taking the piss, right?'

'No, I tell you. Got another baby.'

'You can swap babies?'

Coach Silva laughed. 'Not for free, you bugger. My new baby has fair skin. A costly thing these days. Thus, I eat less.'

Jayanetti wiped sweat off his glasses. Kicked away a coconut shell, shaking his head as he did so. Pointed at Prabu. 'Is he going to threaten Indika's selection for the Sri Lanka Under-seventeens?'

'You see, the thing is—' Coach Silva scrunched up his layered face in Prabu's direction. 'I have to recommend one bowler, one batsman. That's all. Definitely can't recommend two opening batsmen.'

Jayanetti put a hand on Prabu's head. 'Kid's a wizard with a bat in hand.'

'Like Hairy Potter,' Coach Silva said.

'Maybe my boy needs to bowl instead,' Jayanetti said.

'Why's that?' Indika pushed in front of Prabu. 'You think I'm not good enough?'

'Not being serious, putha.'

Coach Silva laughed. 'Your father's my special friend.
I'll work something out.'

'With all due respect, sir,' Indika said, 'I don't want
favours.'

'Everyone wants favours, putha,' Coach Silva said.
'This is Sri Lanka.'

Prabu spoke to the BBC with his lips close together, hiding
those gaps in his teeth.

'How did you bat like that?' the BBC asked him.

'I see the ball, I hit the ball. That is my tactic.'

'Where did you learn to play?'

'I learn it at school when I have six years of age. But
last few years our school is bombed and closed. Then I
play cricket in my camp.'

'We assume you were the best,' the BBC said.

'Correct assume.'

'Did you study in English?'

Prabu said, 'No, no, in Tamil. Not since long time have
everyone in local schools learn in your language.'

'But your English is excellent. Where did—'

'From the great English and American authors
such as William Shakespeare, Charles Dickens, Ernest
Hemingway, James Patterson.'

'You like Shakespeare?'

'No.'

The BBC correspondent paused, looked down at some
notes. 'How long did you stay in the IDP camp and how
were conditions?'

'Maybe I stay for a period not more than one year.

Condition is somewhat okay and I make many friends to play the cricket with and that is how I have been given this chance to have a chance.'

The BBC correspondent looked down at his notes again. 'I'm told your late father delivered babies?'

'Correct.'

'He was a doctor?'

'Who?' Prabu asked.

'Your father.'

'No, no. He was a delivery man.'

The BBC man held his breath. 'Your mother?'

'Misplaced her and my sister,' Prabu said. 'Follow, please.' He paced off camera to Indika who sat on the red clay wicket, head tucked between his knees.

Pointing down at him, Prabu said, 'This is my batting partner. Now he is like my brother.'

'Brither?' the BBC asked.

'Yes, brother. I could not bat that way without his support. You know what is a prom?'

'Yes,' said the BBC. 'American thing.'

'This school I am to join is have a prom call the Papadum. Brother Indika have been prom king, Papadum King, since the Grade Nine.'

Indika, head still between his knees, raised his hand. 'Grade Eight actually.'

Prabu was disappointed he got something wrong. Even though he had no idea how he knew any of this.

FIVE

The sun set over the Monsoon Lodge's colonial clubhouse. The sky, dark with grey clouds, reddened closer to sea level. A train limped past between the club wall and the rock barriers against the sea. Crammed passengers hung out of doors and windows, waving and whistling at sunburnt foreigners sipping gin-and-tonics on an elevated terrace.

Hands in the pockets of Carter Sir's hand-me-down jeans, Prabu sauntered amongst the tables until he spotted his teammate on the lawn below.

Indika sat under a thatched umbrella wearing a batik shirt over jeans with rips across both knees. Tucking his fringe behind his ears, he sucked on a Marlboro Red. Coughed through the smoke. 'Has anyone got anything stronger than this shit?'

A blonde and a brunette sat on either side of him, each with a hand tucked behind his back.

Brunette said, 'You. Find. These. Mild?'

'In Paris I smoked Gitanes with no filters.' Indika lifted two fingers to his lips, closed his eyes. 'The flavour.'

Prabu tapped Indika on his back.

'What the—' Indika said.

'Bro, your jeans are old?' Prabu asked.

'Wait, wait,' Indika said. 'You're a member here?'

Prabu giggled.

Indika grabbed his arm. 'Dude, why you here?'

Wobbling his head around, Prabu grinned so hard he looked constipated. 'For your party time.'

Indika extended his arms out by his side. 'How'd you know I'd be here?'

'You told.'

'Did I? Honestly can't remember.'

'I think maybe you have been take the many alcohols. You told to me also and Gayan, Rajiv and Gish.'

'Yeah I told them, but …' Indika closed his eyes. 'Okay, okay, now you're here, sit, sit.'

A girl with wet hair, tan highlighted by a white bikini top, skipped up to Indika. 'Oh. My. God.' She grabbed his wrists. 'It's been too long.'

Laughing, Indika pointed at Prabu. 'Fiona, meet my new, what would I call him, friend?'

Prabu offered his hand. 'Pleased to be meeting you.'

Resting her hands on Prabu's shoulders, Fiona leaned forward to kiss him on either cheek.

Prabu froze, feet stuck in the grass, jaw locked. He'd heard foreign girls were forward, but kissing him before she knew his name? Wow. He straightened his back, combed his hair down into a side parting, deepened his voice. 'My name is called the Prabu.'

'Pleasure,' she said.

'Fiona is my ex,' Indika said.

Prabu lifted his shoulders. 'I don't follow.'

'We used to date.'

'Date what?'

Indika laughed. 'Dude, she used to be my girlfriend.'

Prabu threw his hand to his mouth to catch the tiny chunk of dhal that he threw up. He pulled the triangularly folded paper serviette out of his shirt pocket. Wiped his cheeks with it. Had to get rid of Fiona's kiss. Crouching down, he raised his hands up in prayer to Indika. 'I must many times make the apologize, my brother. When I accepted her proposal, I was not aware—'

'That was my proposal?' Fiona asked.

Prabu back on his feet. 'I'm sorry, lady. Where I come from, never would we make any action with the lady of a friend, even if their affair had been ended.'

She said, 'But I—'

Prabu's palm up near her face. 'Please, lady. You are beauty, but do not complex this further.'

'Yes, Fiona, you tart,' Indika said, not even trying to hide his laughter. 'Listen to the man.'

'We can be friends, lady,' Prabu said. 'Nothing more, okay?'

Fiona put on a stern face. 'I think that would be for the best.'

'Anyway, people.' Indika stretched his arms above his head. 'I'm going to grab this bottle of arrack, packet of smokes and head over to the other side of the pool with my boy Prabu to discuss tactics for our game on Monday. Back when the bottle's empty.'

'I am not familiar with the consumption of alcohol,' Prabu said.

'Well then, maybe, just maybe, you'll tell me all your secrets,' Indika said. 'Do you have any secrets?'

The boys settled on a bank of sunbeds, next to a wall topped with broken glass lined up like a shark's teeth. The breeze picked up, spraying them with seawater from across the rocks. Indika slouched down, pulled his shirt off over his head. Lit a smoke.

Prabu crossed his arms and watched the sun fizz out into the Indian Ocean. He reached out to accept the arrack from his pal. Glugged it straight from the bottle, spitting some of it out when it burnt his throat. 'Paining, paining.'

Indika laughed. 'Good shit, no?'

'Certainly, shit,' Prabu said. 'Oh Jesus H. Christ. I feel …' Prabu pulled at his own hair, watched the pool swim past him as palm trees frowned. 'I feel good.'

He collapsed on to a sunbed.

SIX

Okay, okay, I can see you now. I missed this part before. Tried to avoid seeing you during the war.

But it's important that I do, I'm told.

You're back at the Panthers' camp, sitting there, doing your work, waiting for Amma.

She promised she'd be back but it's been four days. No sign of her.

Tarzan Subramanium promised to check on you, and here he is. Here's the man with the strong jaw. The man who looks in control. A man you think you can trust.

So I see you sit upright when he enters the Panthers' camp. He passes through the assembly hall, doffing his cap at his colleagues, lifting his hands up in prayer to his elders. But you can see his eyes darting to where you are. You know he's here for you.

And what a greeting he gives you. Runs the last few steps to you. Hugs you, lifting you off the ground. 'Little man, little man,' he says.

'Amma didn't come,' you say.

He leans back, smiles, nods. An I-told-you-so nod. A you-can-trust-me smile.

And at this moment, you have no one else, so Tarzan becomes your mother, your father, your sister, your friend. Other men in the camp are too damn busy with their own kids. Other women too. But here's Tarzan and you're his number one priority. Hell, he makes you feel like you're the only thing in his life.

'Going fishing now,' he says. 'Want to come?'

'On camp?'

He laughs. Whacks you pretty hard on the back. 'Need water to fish, little man.'

'The sea?'

'The sea, little man.'

'I don't like boats,' you say.

'We go in a boat, we'll be shot out of the water, my friend. I fish on stilts.'

'In the sea?'

'Yes.' He shakes his head. 'Need water, remember?'

'And you want me to come too?'

He claps his hands. 'I thought you'd jump at the chance to get off camp.'

'You can get me off the camp?'

'I'm Tarzan.' He thumps his chest. 'Me lord of the jungle. Of course I can.'

'I can't swim,' you say.

'Well then you sit on the beach while I'm on my stilt.'

The beach is pure gold. The finest of sands. The calmest of seas. When Tarzan enters the water and wades to his stilt, you can see his feet all the way. The water is that clear.

Clear enough, you think, to be able to pluck fish out with your hands, but Tarzan uses a rod. Within seconds he has caught his first fish. Tosses it to you on the beach. You try to catch it between your hands but it slips through and flaps about on the sand.

Before you get it into the bucket of water, another fish is flying through the air at you, Tarzan laughing in the background.

Then another, and before you know it, Tarzan is done.

And he calls you to sit with him in the shallowest of water. Tarzan looking at you, a tear in his eye.

Your heart stops. You wonder why he's looking at you like that. Like he wants something from you that you don't want to give him. You turn away but he grabs your chin, making you look straight at him.

'Face just like my boy's.' He slaps his hand against the water. 'Just like …'

'Your son?' you ask, but he doesn't answer. You try again. 'How old is he?'

'He was fourteen.'

'And now he is?'

Tarzan raises an open palm above your face. As if to hit you, but he strokes your hair. 'He's dead.'

You want to know how he died, but Appa would have said it's wrong to ask.

'Shot in combat.' Tarzan covers his face with his hands. 'Defending our women and children. Defending children his own age.'

'Why?' you ask. Could mean anything.

'Why was he fighting?' Tarzan asks. 'Because I was too weak to stand up for him. Because I made a mistake.'

'You think kids shouldn't be fighting?'

'Not my kids, that's for sure.' He skims a shell across the water. 'I saw him, bullet in the chest, dead. I saw him with no breath in him.'

'I'm sorry.'

'No, I'm glad I saw him like that. Otherwise, like you with your family, I'd keep dreaming of him alive when I know he's dead.'

Tarzan has you in the sidecar of his motorbike. You're bumping over mud roads, into and out of giant potholes. Maybe he can't hear you over the noise of the engine. Maybe that's why he's ignoring your questions. Not telling you where you're going. Not telling you why.

He stops the bike at the bottom of a hill. Asks you to follow him up to the top. When you get to the top, you look down and see kids your age, running around. Hundreds of kids, boys and girls.

Jumping through hoops. Swimming across a stream, climbing frames, skipping rope, swinging off trees.

You want to join in. Be with kids your age, playing.

But, just in time, you notice that none of the children are smiling.

SEVEN

Waves crashed into the rocks, sprayed salt water over the walls. Prabu awoke under a thatched umbrella. Alone, like a sentry. Responsible for the safety of others, but scared.

Sitting up, he saw the main bar, packed with men and women in expensive clothes.

A rustling noise made him jump up and into a puddle of vomited rice and carrots. Indika, shirtless, lay by his feet.

Breathing more steadily now, Prabu leaned down. Put his hand under Indika's head. 'What happened, brother?'

Indika blinked slowly. 'The hell are we?'

'Monsoon Lodge Club. By the pool.'

'Do I know you?'

Prabu rubbed his palm across Indika's forehead. Pushed back the hair from in front of his eyes. 'It's me.'

'I know, dude. Oh man, I'm buggered. You passed out?'

'I did, my brother. You make a vomit, no?'

Indika held his head. Laughed. Held his head again. 'That was you, machan.'

'Really, then I must have make a vomit on to your mouth.' Prabu rubbed a finger across Indika's chin.

Indika slapped his hand away. 'Don't tell anyone, okay?'

'You have my promise, brother.' Prabu spotted the arrack, lifting it up to show that about 550ml out of the original 750ml was still in the bottle. 'Shit the pants, we have not drink much.'

Rubbing his temples, Indika sat up. 'Must be another bottle.'

'This is all, my brother.'

Indika snatched the arrack from Prabu, unscrewed the top. Poured it all into the grass. 'Dude, you want to be my friend, you tell everyone we finished this whole bottle, okay?'

'Okay.'

Standing, Indika took off his shoes and trousers. 'Well, come on then.'

Prabu lifted his hand up. Shook his palm at Indika. 'Hey brother, I just want to be friends.'

Indika laughed until he had to grab his head again. Wearing just his boxers, he took a running dive into the deep end of the swimming pool. Returning to the surface, he slapped the back of his hand against the water, aiming the resulting splash at Prabu. 'Machan, I just wanted you to come for a swim. Don't know what used to happen to you gay boys back in Jaffna—'

'I'm from Paddanichchipilayankululm.'

'That's just a noise.' Indika's eyebrows arched. 'What the hell'd you just say?'

'That's where I have reside before.'

'Not drunk enough, dude, if you can still say that name.' Indika took a mouthful of water. Spat it out in Prabu's direction. 'Jump in.'

'The purpose of my reluctance is that I am unfamiliar with the deep end when swimming.'

'You can't swim?' Indika asked.

'They train me in flotation, but I am not so much confident.'

Swimming breaststroke, Indika bisected the reflection of the moon in the water. He waved Prabu towards the shallow end.

Prabu took off his shirt, and when he unbuckled his belt, his borrowed jeans fell right off him.

'Jesus,' Indika said. 'Those are the smallest underpants I've ever seen on a man.'

'My uncle gave them to me, because they became too much small for him.'

'Is your uncle, like, ten years old?'

'Yes.'

Indika almost pissed himself laughing. 'I'm not going to ask. Just get in before people think you're naked.'

Prabu kissed the pendant hanging from his neck. Lifted his hands to his mouth, up to the sky, closed his eyes, chanted in Tamil. Held his nose before jumping in.

As soon as his head went underwater, Prabu knew he would die. Flapping his arms, he sucked in what he hoped was air. Instead, chlorinated water.

In time, he realized that he could actually stand so he allowed his shouts and screams to whimper out as he surfaced with chemically treated water dribbling out of his mouth.

Indika reached out to him. 'You've been brought up in the warzones, right?'

'Correct,' Prabu said, dragging up his little underpants. 'Prior to the war ending.'

'So you've seen bombs, landmines, gunfire? Things like that?'

Prabu held on to the side of the pool. 'Every day. Maybe more.'

Indika's hands above the water. 'And you're scared of jumping into a pool?'

'Astrologer told to my mother that maybe I would meet my death in water. Result, I remain committed to a fear of swimming.'

'We're just standing, dude. Don't worry.' Indika crouched into the water. Squinting, he pointed up the slope towards the clubhouse. 'You see that girl coming in?'

'My shits, she is a hot like a waitress,' Prabu said.

The girl, at about five foot five, was taller than the boy she was with. Looking out over the club's cascade into the sea, she repeatedly brushed her hand through her blonde highlighted hair. Appearing to struggle with the tightness of her black dress as she sat down, she crossed her arms in front of her breasts. Breasts the likes of which Prabu had only seen in sketches. Her skin, the colour of coffee ice cream, made the boy she was with look almost too dark to be noticed at night.

'Isabella,' Indika said. 'Half English, half Sri Lankan. I really, really want to snog her.'

'What you want to do to her?' Prabu dropped his head to one side. 'Smock?'

'Snog, you know. Means kiss.'

'Oh yes.' Prabu let out a schoolgirl giggle. 'She certainly is worth for a kiss. Maybe more.'

Indika smacked his hand down against the surface of the pool water. 'But she's going out with that punk apparently.'

'He have the same face to the wicketkeeper from our game today.'

'Yeah, dude, it's his brother. Remember? Calls himself Shock Ice.'

Shock Ice wore baggy jeans buckled around his hip bones, showing red boxer shorts. Strutted like a bodybuilder, thrusting his flabby chest out in a camouflage tanktop. He wore large gold chains around his neck. A baseball cap back to front.

'What a jackasshole.' Prabu scrunched up his nose. 'Why she is with him?'

'Didn't know she was. Clearly just interested in his flash car and bodyguards. Thought better of her.'

Shock Ice sat at a table opposite Isabella. His five bodyguards jostled around testing the champagne and butter-fried cuttlefish for him.

Indika and Prabu dripped their way back to the sunbeds, dressing without drying themselves.

'Rub your hands against the side of your jeans,' Indika said, passing Prabu a cigarette.

Holding it between his thumb and forefinger, Prabu

sucked in the smoke, coughing more out than seemed to go in.

'You're not inhaling, machan,' Indika said. 'Take it into your throat.' With his gaze locked on Isabella, he poured two glasses of arrack, Prabu's much the larger.

'Watch this.' Indika pulled out his phone, dialling a number. Shock Ice's phone rang to the theme of 'You're Beautiful' by James Blunt.

He answered. 'Wassap?'

Indika hung up. 'Have his number because he once called me asking if I knew any white chicks.'

Prabu ducked under the table. 'Shit the panties. Then he know you are person who called that call.'

'Called the ... No, dude, my number doesn't show up. Just says private number.' Indika took a sip of arrack, threw a hand to his mouth. Bolted off in the direction of the changing rooms.

A loud, high-pitched shout from the bar deck.

Shock Ice stood up. Back-heeled his chair away. Pounding himself on the chest with his fist, he spat at Isabella's feet, pissed off out of there.

The bodyguards stormed after him, leaving a waiter standing with an open bottle of Moet in his hands.

Isabella listened to what the waiters had to say, nodding her head as they spoke. She waved at Prabu, tripping over her high heels as she walked towards him.

'Is Indika with you?' she asked in an accent that Prabu thought was a bit like Mr Carter's but not quite.

He smiled and grunted, looking down her cleavage

before he realized he had done so. Unable to speak, he rolled his head to say yes.

The next few moments were a blur. The greatest thing to ever happen to him, but the worst thing possible for his friendship with Indika.

Indika returned, rocking heavily from one foot to the other, his hair slicked back with extra water. 'What did Isabella want?'

Prabu, head bowed, grabbed him by the shoulders. 'I am many sorry, my friend.'

Indika's eyebrows merged as he fell back into a chair.

'I know you love this Isabella, and why not?' Prabu said. 'She is even more beauty when you see her closer. But brother, she is not right for you.'

'What the hell have you been drinking?' Indika asked.

'Arrack.' Prabu shook his head and picked up a bottle. 'Remember?'

'What did she want?'

'First she telled to me that you are a friend of hers. Then she made an accuse that Shock Ice left without pay the bill.'

'Yeah, I saw that.'

'Well, the bill is very big one.'

'She wanted money?' Indika asked. 'Doesn't surprise—'

'No, she can give money. She said, because she is not a member of the club she could not make a pay as pay is only made on an account credit basis. She said you can sign and she could pay you the money.'

'Why the hell would she pay for that animal, though?'

'The waiters otherwise have to pay,' Prabu said. 'And he does this oftentimes methinking. Methinking confirmed by what she told to me.'

'Yeah, okay, I'll sign.' Indika rubbed at a pimple on his nose. 'But I don't want to meet her now.'

'So you saw?' Prabu asked.

'Saw what?'

'I must inform you with many different types of apologize that she snogged me before she left.'

Indika's head turned so fast his neck made a clicking noise. Snapping back on to his feet, he leaned into Prabu. 'She snogged you?'

'Yes, brother, but I did not return said snog.'

'She bloody snogged you?'

'Brother, I pushed her away. I told her of your love for her and—'

Indika grabbed Prabu by his shirt, so wet it dripped blue dye. 'You snogged her? Told her I loved her?' Indika crouched behind the table, burying his head in his arms. 'Life has ended.'

'I must make to you an apologize, because she is look very upset when I said my lips were yours.'

'You said your lips were mine?' Indika grabbed his own hair. 'You want her to think we're gay? You said your lips were mine?'

'When you say it like that, it does sound maybe gay.'

'How did you say it?'

'Exactly like that.'

Indika closed his eyes. 'You snogged her, told her I love her, then said your lips were mine? Ah, Jesus.' Shaking his head, Indika picked up his cigarettes. 'I'm going to the bar. Better you go home.'

Prabu sat still for a few minutes. Did some thinking. Thought he needed to make it up to Indika. Hurrying up the stairs to the bar, he looked through the window. Saw Indika at a table with the six founding members of the most feared gang in his year group, the Scorpion Five.

He felt like he was rising off the ground when Indika made eye contact with him. Holding one hand to his chest and pointing at Indika's table with the other, he mouthed the words, 'Shall I come in?'

Indika shook his head. 'Go.'

A tear shot down Prabu's face into his mouth. He looked at his feet and shuffled away.

He sat down at the entrance on an ornamental brass cannon, waiting to make sure that Indika didn't get too drunk to find his way home.

EIGHT

BMWs and Range Rovers shared rows with trishaws and white vans. Lined up like toy cars, dropped randomly from above. No attention paid to designated parking spaces.

Three security guards stood watch at the front gate. Sharing smokes with eight or nine drivers, some in sarongs, some in uniform. On the other side of the wall, armed policemen guarded the road outside Araliya Temple, the prime minister's house.

Prabu watched the guards lift the barrier to the car park. Three jeeps, their headlights darting, rumbled right up to the cannon Prabu sat on.

Four men in black trousers and white shirts talked to each other on walkie-talkies even though they were close enough to hold hands. They opened the driver's door of the middle jeep, out of which climbed Shock Ice, speaking into his BlackBerry.

Two of the bodyguards, one of them with fresh blood on his polished boots, approached the club receptionist and asked questions that the receptionist could not answer.

Prabu ambled towards them, asked them what they wanted.

The men flashed Bollywood villain snarls. One said, 'We are looking for Prabu.'

Thumping his chest, Prabu said, 'That is me.'

The men bent over, grabbing Prabu under his armpits. They dragged him to the circular lawn in the middle of the car park. Stopped in front of Shock Ice who punched Prabu bang in the middle of his six-pack, forcing him to spit out remnants of arrack on his own rubber slippers.

Shock Ice put his BlackBerry screen up to Prabu's face. 'Got me this SMS from some nigger hollering at me that a Tamil punk snogged ma bitch. This true?'

Prabu made eye contact. 'Who is said bitch?'

'Don't you play them games with me, nigger boy. You know I is with Isabella.'

Appa always told Prabu not to lie. Unless necessary. 'She put two snogs on me.'

Shock Ice pulled out a pistol from the back of his jeans. Passing it to a bodyguard, he threw six slaps across Prabu's face, two of which hurt.

Holding his breath. Holding his urge to pull this guy's eyes out. Prabu grinned.

This pissed off the biggest bodyguard, who kicked at Prabu's ankles, dropping him to the grass. Prabu landed ass first, a butt cheek on either side of an elevated tree root.

He turned to face the crowd forming by the ornamental cannon. Indika stood at the back, stooping so low Prabu struggled to see him.

Isabella pushed her way through the crowd. 'You bloody coward,' she said to Shock Ice, now sitting on Prabu's chest.

Two men grabbed her from behind, pulling her hair.

'You need bodyguards to hold a girl back?' she asked. 'Get. Off. Him.'

Shock Ice spat right in between Prabu's eyes.

And Prabu saw flashes of himself in combat gear. Standing over the body of a dead soldier. Over the bodies of dead kids. He didn't understand these visions. Couldn't control them. Could only control himself even though he knew he could snap Shock Ice's neck in a second.

Laughing, Shock Ice dropped a stone on Prabu's head, causing blood to flow out of his ear like melted ice cream from a crack in a cone.

On his feet, the punk turned to Isabella. 'Well, if it ain't the bitch slut who got a jiggy jiggy with the nigger.'

Isabella spat at him. 'You dweeb-little-turd-punk-ass-mother–'

Shock Ice strode towards Isabella. Slapped her flush across the face.

This was getting harder for Prabu. Harder to control. He arched his back and kicked out his legs, landing on his feet in front of Shock Ice. He planned to headbutt the bridge of the bastard's nose until …

'No, no, no,' Isabella said. 'Don't act like them.'

Prabu stood still as Shock Ice threw a punch at him. It didn't hurt, but Prabu dropped to the ground. Let his legs go.

The bodyguards pulled out guns, 'Shall we shoot?'

Indika and the rest of the crowd gasped like a pantomime audience.

But Prabu grinned. An almost toothless grin.

Shock Ice backed away. As if he'd seen a ghost. Turned towards the crowd, looking at people with phones filming what was happening. Pointing to another bodyguard, he said, 'Boom Boom, take every nigger's phone. Every nigger.' He shuffled his feet, big right step, small left step, dropping his shoulder as he moved. 'I ain't gonna lie to you dawgs. I'm a bad mother. You know who I am, I is know who all you bitches are and where you live at. I don't want to see any of this go viral.'

Her hands constrained by the thugs, Isabella pointed at Prabu with her chin. 'What the hell did he do to deserve this?'

'He did you, bitch queen.'

Shaking her shoulders in a vain effort to get free, Isabella breathed in. 'What. Are. You. Talking. About?'

Prabu knew she'd try to deny it. Knew she had to.

Shock Ice spat at her lips. 'You're ma bitch and you diss me by snogging this little nigger.'

'Who told you that?'

'Got me a text, didn't I?' Shock Ice said.

Indika, looking down, back-pedalled further into the crowd.

'Text from a private number done tell me that some nigger, goes by the name of Prabu, he be snogging on ma bitch.'

'First of all, I am not yours or anybody's bitch. Secondly, stop trying to be gangster, you little twat.'

Isabella pushed away from the bodyguards. 'Thirdly, I didn't snog this boy.'

Prabu understood the need to lie. But it embarrassed him. Still hurt.

Shock Ice said, 'Mountain Man, bring the nigger boy here.'

Dragging him by his arms, Mountain Man planted Prabu on his feet.

'Tell me what you is told me before, little nigger boy. You snog anyone tonight?'

Prabu looked down at his feet. 'Two girls snogged me tonight.'

'Who them girls done snog you, nigger?'

Prabu looked towards the crowd gathered by the entrance to the clubhouse. 'One white-coloured girl, I can't see. I think she have the parted.'

'The white girl and the nigger boy,' Shock Ice said. 'The second girl?'

Prabu looked at Indika, spat out blood, said, 'Sorry, my brother.' He pointed at Isabella. 'She snogged me.'

'What?' Isabella said. 'What the hell have you been drinking?'

'Arrack,' Prabu said. 'When you came to my table, after you is saying bye, you gave to me two snogs.'

Isabella looked up at the branches of the banyan tree, shook her head. 'I kissed you on the cheeks, Prabu. I kissed you on the cheeks. Is that what this is all about? Two kisses on the cheek?'

'I ain't no bloody idiot,' said Shock Ice.

'Then you do a very good impression,' Isabella said.

Shock Ice's hand up in Isabella's face, he turned to Prabu. 'Nigger, you ain't saying she kissed you on the cheeks? You ain't saying them girls who snogged you, just done kiss you on the cheeks?'

'That's a snog, no?' Prabu said. 'A kiss is a snog?'

'Was there tongue?' Shock Ice asked.

'Yes, they both had tongues.'

Grabbing Prabu's neck, Shock Ice asked, 'Did them bitches use them?'

Prabu closed his eyes. 'No.'

'I am sorry, black boy, I don't hear you. What you say?'

'No.'

Isabella pointed towards Prabu, said, 'He needs a doctor.'

'Yo, Isabeauty.' Shock Ice tugged at Isabella's arm. 'It seems we been rapping different songs here, babe. You know, I mean–'

She wriggled free from his grip. Pushed him away. 'Don't you ever speak to me again.'

'Listen, you go kissing Tamils on the cheek, I reconsider the status of our relationship.'

'There is no bloody relationship.'

'On Facebook, I'll say it's complicated.' Shock Ice moved towards Isabella. Punched her in the gut. She fell to the ground, hitting her head on the roots of the banyan tree. Prabu slithered out of the bodyguard's grip. Got his arms round Shock Ice's throat. And he knew. Somehow he knew where to squeeze the life out of him. How to kill him.

And he tasted blood in his mouth. Shit between his

teeth, salt water in his eyes. The smell of rotting flesh, the sounds of choppers and mortar fire.

What the hell was going on in his head?

Mountain Man pistol-whipped Prabu to the floor. Saving him from making a ridiculous mistake.

From the grass, once she could breathe, Isabella said, 'Leave. Him. Alone.'

Shock Ice picked up a stone, chucked it at her. Missed. 'You see another man, I know, and I kick your beauty booty.'

'I'm a British citizen, you forget. I can leave the country any time. Nothing you can do.'

'Try me, biatch,' Shock Ice said, lighting a cigar, laughing. Strutting to his jeep. Coughing. 'Try me.'

The thugs spat at Prabu, scurried after Shock Ice, jumped into the last jeep as it screeched through the gate.

Isabella lay next to Prabu, looked at the crowd, said, 'Who the hell told this hooligan I'd snogged you?'

Prabu said, 'Maybe someone is seeing?'

'But nothing happened, so there was nothing to see. Did you tell ...'

Prabu glared at Indika as he turned away. 'No, I did tell no one.'

NINE

I see Tarzan Subramanium smiling. Looking at you. 'You want to join them?'

You know what this is and it isn't kids having a run around. Having fun.

'But, what is ... Is this a training camp?'

'It's not what you think, little man.' Tarzan squats. Lights a cigarette, makes a shell shape with his hands and sucks the smoke out of that. 'You're right, it's a training camp, but not for soldiers.'

'These kids aren't soldiers?'

'No, not soldiers,' he says. 'Just here to get fit. Get strong, so if the Sinhalese bastards attack their villages, they can run. They can hide. They can survive. Make sense?'

'Well ...'

'If you run, little man, could you hide in the jungle? Live in the jungle?'

'Would I have to?' you ask.

'Maybe.' Tarzan sucks in more smoke. 'So you should

be prepared. You're coming with me.' Tarzan grabs your
hand and pulls you down a loose stone path to the bottom
of the hill. 'This is a Panther camp.'

You understand his logic, but you're scared. Bloody
scared. 'But what if I don't like it?'

'Try today, try tomorrow. If you don't like it, you come
straight back with me. If you do like it, you stay a week
or two and I'll come back for you.'

The camp is underground, down fifteen steps: a friggin'
air-conditioned bunker. The Supreme Leader of the
Panthers sucks smoke from a cigar. Rubs his rice-belly.
Nods towards Tarzan.

Each time he speaks, his shoulders rock up and down,
his moustache twitches. He appears to be laughing all the
time. Maybe that's just his face. His demeanour.

He doesn't have the presence you expected. He's not as
scary as you thought he might be. Maybe that's because
he's buddy-buddy with Tarzan, and you trust Tarzan.

Chubby cheeks, cauliflower ears, slightly red eyes and
chipped teeth, the Supreme Leader looks a bit like an evil
clown. Dressed in gym shorts and a skinny that is far too
skinny for him.

'I got films for you to watch.' He looks straight at
you. 'I guess you haven't watched movies for a while.
So tonight, the video room's all yours.' He cups your
chin, kisses your forehead with surprisingly moist lips.
'My favourite's *Death Wish*, but hell, I like all Charles
Bronson films.'

Death Wish is a film about a man who goes on a rampage when his wife is murdered and his daughter raped by muggers. The Supreme Leader, it is said, calls himself a vigilante. Avenging the murder of his wife by a government soldier. They say he broke away from the Tigers because they started peace talks.

The slogan on the wall: 'We never make peace with murderers.'

It's midnight by the time you finish watching. You share a tattered rattan mat with four other younger and hungrier boys. Barely sleep. Up at four-thirty in the morning for your first day of training.

A man with a moustache runs his hands over his blubbery red lips. Throws a uniform at your feet. 'Wear these with pride.'

His name's Machine Gun Kelly. Named after a Charles Bronson film like everyone senior in this damn place – except Tarzan.

Your uniform's too tight. You struggle to pull up the combat trousers, the top button remains open. The shirt's a better fit but it has a bullet hole and a bloodstain right next to your heart. The hat's peak is square like the ones sported by the dudes that visited your appa before he vanished.

You pull the peak down to cover your eyes so you don't have to look at anyone.

'We're short of shoes,' Machine Gun Kelly says. 'So we'll train barefoot.'

The first task is like hurdles. A race. Twenty-three of you cats, ranging in age from eleven to fifteen. There are low hurdles, but they get progressively higher, the last of them around the level of your chest.

You cream the field. Win the race at a friggin' canter.

'Some of you are much older than this boy,' Machine Gun Kelly says. 'Disgrace.'

The next race, crawling on stomachs under barbed wire, through pits that stink of rotting flesh. After that, monkey bars, jumps over blazing tyres.

Then cartwheels. Forward rolls. Press-ups with one arm on either side of parallel bars. You're the only bugger who can do more than three. You do 102.

Then, walking across ropes tied from one coconut tree to another. Twenty feet in the air, Mr Majestyk shaking the friggin' tree. You shit yourself but more through fear of not finishing. Of failing. Of letting Tarzan down.

You break for lunch, if you can call it that. Slush, a bit of rice, some rotting bananas. Machine Gun Kelly and his assistants eat better stuff. Fresh stuff.

After lunch it's water training, and you hate water.

You're given sticks and told to carry them like guns.

'Jump in,' Mr Majestyk says.

You hesitate. The water is murky, muddy. Can't see into it. Could be anything under there.

'Jump in, you little pricks,' Murphy's Law says.

He kicks you in the gap between your ass cheeks. You bellyflop into the water.

You crawl straight out, coughing up mud. Met by Mr Majestyk's boots. He swings a kick within inches of your face.

'Where's your gun?'

'My gun, sir?'

'That stick, you dumb cock.' Murphy's Law brushes the sole of his boots across your ass, rolling you back into the water. 'Never leave your gun, idiot.'

You're underwater and can't swim but the river is shallow, so you push off the muddy bed and your head breaks the surface.

'Your gun?' Mr Majestyk shouts. 'Where the hell is your gun?'

'Don't know.'

Muphy's Law lifts his rifle. You duck back under. Know you can't surface again without the stick. You brush your palms across the bed of the river but can't find anything. No stick, but your hands are sinking and you can't breathe.

You grab the stick out of the hand of the boy standing next to you. Lift it above your head. 'Here's my gun.'

'And yours?' Mr Majestyk asks the boy next to you.

'Sir, he took it.'

'Come here,' says Murphy's Law. He grabs the boy by his neck. Lifts him up against a tree. 'The only thing worse than losing your gun is letting someone else get it from you.'

He swings the boy against a branch. 'Stay out here tonight.'

'The rest of you,' Machine Gun Kelly says, 'back to the dorm.'

The dorm's a metal structure on which there was probably once a roof but not now. Music plays in the background and names are called. Each kid is presented with something, which is placed around his or her neck.

You wonder what it is, but your name's never called.

You have a bad feeling about this place so you look for Tarzan. You'll go with him, away from this place. Far away.

But when you ask where he is, Murphy's Law lights a match. 'Just like this' – he blows it out – 'he's gone.'

TEN

A man in a vest bounced along on the driver's seat to the tuk-tukking noises of the trishaw. Indika, Prabu, Isabella in the back.

Prabu tried to watch the road. Buses and motorcycles circled around his head. He had to close his eyes. 'Drank too much arrack.'

Isabella put a hand on his thigh. 'It's more than that.'

A policeman in a crash helmet ran out on to the road, waving his arms around. The trishaw's engine spluttered to a stop, the driver got out, grinning so much his upper lip touched his nose. He handed over his driver's licence and wobbled his head around.

Another cop, over sixty, waterbed-belly, creases under his eyes, limped to the trishaw, said, 'ID.'

Prabu cupped his hands around his mouth, blew out and faced the other way.

'Boss,' Indika said, 'we really need to get my friend to hospital.'

The policeman kept saying something in Sinhala, until Indika said, in Sinhala, that he couldn't speak Sinhala.

'You been drink the alcohol?' the policeman asked.

Isabella and Indika nodded.

'How old you?'

'Sixteen, she's seventeen,' Indika said.

'Too young to drink the alcohol.' He jabbed his open palm into the trishaw again. 'ID.'

Indika and Isabella handed over their cards. Prabu opened his wallet to see if he had anything that could pass for identification, eventually settling on a photograph of him with Appa, Amma and Akka.

The policeman placed Indika's and Isabella's ID cards in his shirt pocket, looked down at Prabu's photograph. He called over another policeman. One almost as high-pitched as the other, they giggled nonstop, for just short of three minutes. Prabu timed it.

'This not ID. This picture of you and other Tamils.'

Prabu rolled his head.

'One father, one mother, one sister? What your father is doing for job?'

Vision locked on the main cop, Prabu said, 'Delivers babies.'

'Ah a peon. Not clever to travel, as Tamil, without ID. Now you all drink without having the age. You know what is punishment for drinking?'

'A hangover?' Isabella asked.

'Don't test him, babe,' Indika said. 'Get out, come on.'

Prabu clambered out with Isabella's help.

The main cop, appearing senior in that he wore a hat rather than a helmet, draped his arms over Prabu's and Indika's shoulders, then gazed up and down Isabella's bare legs. 'What shall I do?'

Prabu said, 'Maybe can let us go and we promise next time we not drink and I carry ID.'

'I have to report,' the cop said. 'This my job. Then maybe you must go court and it take lot of money and time to release. Very difficult for you. Maybe pay fine also.'

'We can't pay the fine now?' Indika asked.

The cop smiled, released his grip on their shoulders. Spoke to the other policeman in Sinhala. Turning back, said, 'Normally must pay fine at court. We not allowed to take the payments. What we can do?'

Indika placed a hand on the main cop's back. 'Can you pay the fine for us?'

After conferring with the other policeman again, the main cop said, 'This not correct. But I like you. You remind me of a memory. Maybe you give to me the fine, also the transport and tea money?'

'He wants a bloody bribe,' Isabella said.

Prabu understood the signal from Indika. He turned Isabella away to face the trishaw driver, who also looked up and down her legs.

'What shall I do?' the main cop said.

Indika asked, 'How much?'

'For whole package?' The main cop pulled out a calculator, typed in some numbers and handed it to Indika. 'Maybe you give me four thousand?'

'Can't go higher than two, boss.' Indika typed the

numbers into the calculator. 'Boss, my friend needs stitches.'

Snatching the calculator, the cop said, 'Two thousand is for prepaid package.'

'Paying a fine before an offence?'

'Safety first,' the main cop said. 'Because I like you, I can give whole package, three thousand five hundred.' He handed the calculator back to Indika.

'My final offer is three thousand. Good for all of us, no, boss?'

Both cops smiled. 'I lose money. I spend lot of time with you now. Many people I could have stopped and fined. But okay, you my friends, and I like to be nice to Tamil.'

'You take credit cards?' Indika asked, smiling with his eyes.

'Not have that facility yet. Is good idea.'

'Maybe a loyalty card,' Isabella said.

'Loyalty card.' The policeman wrote it down on his notepad.

Prabu handed Indika all his money, the notes crumpled up in a ball.

'This is all you've got? Eighty rupees? Keep it, brother.'

Indika pulled out three thousand rupees from his wallet and handed it to the main cop, who handed it to the junior cop.

'Are you crazy, give the money like that in the open?' The junior cop gave the money back to Indika. 'Place money in your palm, then shake my hand.'

Indika did as told.

The cop looked at the money, rubbed his waterbed-belly, said, 'Come again, please.'

The driver tugged at the lever of the trishaw to get the engine coughing again, but just before he accelerated, the main cop poked his head inside.

Looking directly at Isabella, he said, 'Phone number please, missy.'

Prabu lay on his back while a nurse shaved a semicircle at the front of his hairline.

'You boys been drinking?' The doctor looked too old to still be working. Too shaky to be stitching.

Prabu looked across at Indika sitting next to his bed. 'Somewhat, we finished a bottle of arrack.'

The doctor slapped the back of his hand against his own forehead. 'Your parents deserve this if they let you roam the streets at your age.' He put his tools down. 'Done. Now piss off.'

Prabu sat up, asked Indika, 'Do I still look like a sexy?'

Indika bent over the bed, said, 'You look ...' He spat out the chewing gum from his mouth, fell forward and came up purple, still catching his breath. 'You look utterly ridiculous.'

'Not a sexy, then?'

Indika pushed Prabu in a wheelchair towards his father's Range Rover. He stopped and kissed Isabella on the cheeks. 'Your uncle will take you?'

She nodded, bent over to kiss Prabu on the top of his head. 'That's not a snog.' Straightening, she hugged

Indika, breathing in through her nose near his neck. 'I'm going back to London,' she said. 'My uncle agrees it's the only way. It's not like Shock Ice is going to be punished. Going to be controlled.'

'Sorry I didn't come out sooner,' Indika said. 'No one told me Shock Ice was beating on you two.'

Isabella pecked Indika on the lips. 'I'll be in England, babe.'

The Range Rover stopped just off Thimbirigasyaya Road.

Indika's father – Thathi – got out, said, 'This building looks too thin to survive a change in breeze.' He opened the back door for Prabu.

Prabu felt like he was floating. The injection they had given him at the hospital started taking effect. No more pain in his ribs and nose. Didn't even feel his feet touching the road.

He dropped to his knees, on wet asphalt, to kiss Thathi's feet. Rose to place his hand on Indika's lap. 'Thank you, brother.'

He limped towards the front door, knowing he didn't have a key, but hoping the landlord would wake up in a couple of hours. He watched as the jeep started moving away, possibly just in first gear, then he slumped against the wall and closed his eyes.

He heard the jeep reversing. Straightening his legs, he pushed off the wall.

The driver's window was rolled down. Thathi ran his fingers through his curly hair, lowered his glasses and typed out a message on his phone. 'I'm just texting my wife to say you're coming home to stay with us tonight.'

Prabu opened Indika's door, raised a hand to high-five him, but Indika was looking down at his feet, shaking his head, mumbling something.

ELEVEN

A security guard opened the gates, saluted Thathi. Ahead, a driveway like an airstrip. Botanical gardens and swimming pool to the left, fifteen-foot brick wall to the right.

The house was wow. The size of a damn hospital. Open verandas, bamboo blinds, terracotta-tile roof. Wooden-framed glass doors, floor to ceiling around the living room.

Indika's mother – Ammi – dyed brown hair tucked under the arms of thick glasses, waved from an open cement kitchen. Blew kisses, tottered down the cobblestone driveway in slippers, toes freshly painted, a black dog at her feet. 'Where's my little darling?'

Indika checked his phone, whistled while his mother hugged him. 'Enough, already.'

Releasing her son, Ammi slapped the back of one palm against the front of the other. 'Surely we have to do something about these thugs.'

'I'm telling you,' Indika said, 'it's a lawless society.'

'Just a few bad eggs,' Thathi said.

'But they answer to no one?' asked Ammi.

Prabu coughed, hoping to be introduced to this glamorous lady.

Thathi lowered his voice. 'They've got something on the minister of absolute justice. Sure as hell, I tell you.'

'What do you need on a man who was caught at a whorehouse? That's enough, isn't it?'

'Said he thought it was a warehouse,' Thathi said.

'Even the second time?' Ammi asked.

Prabu had given up on attracting attention. Stroked the dog instead.

'This is your friend?' Ammi crouched next to Prabu, a hand on his back.

Indika grunted. 'Name's Prabu.'

'Well Prabu, you have a way with dogs,' Ammi said. 'Sally normally hates strangers.'

Prabu stood up, at attention, raised his hands in prayer. 'Hello, madam.'

Upright, Ammi extended a hand to Prabu, but he dropped to his knees, kissed her feet. Got back up with smudges of mint-candy-apple nail polish on his nose.

Thathi and Indika raised hands to their mouths, their shoulders bouncing.

'I have a dog in my hometown,' Prabu said. 'His name is Toyota because he is white like a Toyota.'

Indika and Thathi turned away. Paced up the lawn.

'I brought for you, madam, a lemon puff.' Prabu pulled the unwrapped biscuit out of his pocket, handed it to her.

'That's so kind.' She held it with the tips of her fingers. 'I'll have this now with a cup of tea. In the meantime, why don't you follow Indika up to his room to freshen up?'

Indika had locked his bedroom door. Didn't answer Prabu's hundred-bang knocking. Maybe his banging wasn't loud enough, but Prabu could hear Indika on the phone, complaining about some dude he couldn't get rid of.

His knuckles started to hurt, so Prabu gave up knocking. Instead, he inched around the house. Came to a large oak door, intricately carved with images of lion claws. His shoulders hurt too much to push the door open with his arms, so he backed into it with his bum.

Inside, he squatted under a brass ceiling-fan that whistled as it rotated.

He looked up at Thathi's bookshelf, stood and reached for a book titled *Black July*. Pulled it out, blew dust off it. Its pages eaten by some bug or other, but the photographs told the stories.

Pictures of naked men, their private parts blurred out. Their heads in their hands. Fully clothed men dancing around them, lighting fires.

Banging drums. Drinking.

Blowing horns Prabu felt he could hear.

'This was long before you or my son were born,' said Thathi, his shadow as black as Prabu.

Prabu cradled the book like a gun. Tried to conceal it. 'I am sorry for be look—'

'Books are there to be shared.' Thathi wobbled his head. A figure of eight. 'If not for books, there's no knowledge. You like reading?'

'I love.'

'May I?' Thathi took the book from Prabu. 'You know what this is about? *Black July*?'

'I have heard those words.'

'But you don't know what they mean?' Thathi slumped down into his chair. Tall-backed, leather, chairman-of-the-boardroom chair. Patted a stool next to him. 'Sit, sit.'

'I am very dirty.' Prabu pointed to the mud stains, the oil stains, the bloodstains. On his shirt, his trousers, his shoes.

Peering at him over his glasses, Thathi said, 'Fine to stand then. Would you like me to tell you about this?' He tapped the book.

Prabu nodded.

'July 1983, the Tigers ... You know who the Tigers are, right?'

'Correct.'

Thathi closed his eyes, nodded. 'The Tigers ambushed and killed thirteen soldiers. Could be said to be the start of it, but the response ... It was the response. Okay, well, when army soldiers are killed, their bodies are sent back to their families. But the authorities worried that there could be incidents in multiple locations.'

Images of coffins flashed before Prabu.

'The president,' Thathi said, 'he wanted all the bodies to be buried in Colombo, with full military honours. The PM, a wise man, name of Premadasa, warned against it. Said this could incite mobs to violence, but the prez insisted.'

Prabu nodded along to show he was listening even though he couldn't understand everything.

'But the families still wanted the bodies, so the bodies weren't taken to the cemetery. Wild rumour, the

Sri Lankan type, spread. Pissed off the crowds and they kicked off some fights with the police and the army, but then things got …'

Prabu could see that Thathi had a tear running down his face. Offered the old man the corner of his t-shirt to wipe his face with, but Thathi waved him away.

'The mob headed to Borella, burnt down a Tamil shop, burnt down Tamil flats, and then started burning down Tamil houses.'

'How they know a house is a Tamil house? A shop is a Tamil shop?' Prabu asked.

'First, just by the names, I guess. But the next day they were armed with the voter's registry. How'd they get that?'

'Ah,' Prabu said. 'I don't know.'

'Speculation someone in the government orchestrated all this, but who knows?'

Prabu had lived in a war. Couldn't remember everything. Just had flashes of death. Of shooting. Never knew why they started fighting. No one told him. Just told him to hate hate hate. Take a breath. Then hate hate hate some more.

'Welikada Prison. Thirty-seven Tamil inmates knifed or clubbed to death by Sinhalese, the wardens just looking on, they say.'

'Jesus.'

'A train on the way to Jaffna, stopped outside Fort station. Sinhalese passengers killed twelve Tamil passengers. I just don't …'

Grown men don't like people to see them cry. Prabu knew this. Knew the shame, so he looked down at his own feet. Held his breath. Peeked at Thathi once or twice.

'I just don't know,' Thathi said, 'how our people could become like that. The anger, the hatred. A supposedly peaceful people. Smilers, jokers. Dancers. I mean, just sheep, following each other to hell. But you know what? You know how they were punished?'

Prabu loved a good vengeance story. 'How, sir?'

'They weren't. That's the thing. To this day, no punishment for the killers, no compensation for the victims. I bet you have cousins living in England, Australia, Canada, India. Refugees, burnt out of their homes.'

'I don't know,' Prabu said.

'But let me tell you the good side, if you can say there is one.' Thathi straightened his back. No longer slouched. 'In my circles we had, I mean we have, a lot of respect for Tamils. They work hard and take pride in what they do. Anywhere in the world, established majorities don't like being threatened by minorities.'

'Tamils were make threats?'

Thathi looked at the book. Stroked the cover. 'What I'm sure you haven't been told is how many good Sinhalese people protected Tamils. Hell, I don't even need to say good Sinhalese. I just mean Sinhalese. Real Sinhalese.'

'What you are mean, sir? Protect?'

Thathi rose to his feet. Opened a glass cabinet out of which he pulled a photo album. 'We had seventeen Tamils staying with us through the riots.' He placed the album on Prabu's lap. Signalled for him to flick through it.

Prabu turned the pages; faded colour pictures of happy people. Skinny, but happy, doing normal things like playing cricket, watching TV, dancing, arms like twigs flapping in the air.

'We hid them. People we knew. People who worked for me. A couple of complete strangers too.'

'But what if the mob is find them in your house?'

'That's the risk we had to take. Back then we didn't have kids, and if we did, I often wonder if I would have put them at risk like that.' Thathi held a finger to his chin, looking up at the ceiling. 'I hope so. How could we shut the door to people? To human beings?'

'You are heroes,' Prabu said.

'Well that's just it,' Thathi said. 'No I'm not. Ammi isn't. We were just a young couple with a large house my in-laws had given us. And we did what every other sane person would do. Did do. The Sinhalese, we're good people.'

'But then what about—'

'We are. My friends all sheltered Tamils. Some got caught. One friend, he lost an eye and an arm trying to stop a mob from taking away his Tamil maid. His maid. I mean, that's a goddamn hero. Another friend, a lady, tried to fight away a mob with a broom to save her Tamil driver.'

Prabu imagined Indika and his family protecting him like that. He felt like he could cry too. Tears down his face.

They sat, in silence, the only noise the click of the brass fan.

'Anyway, that is past now,' Prabu said.

'But is it? Some youngsters just get brainwashed by my generation, and it's important that you don't. That Indika doesn't.'

'We fight together now.'

'You know there's this joke about my generation of Sri Lankans. Not Sinhalese, just Sri Lankans. You like jokes?'

'Please to tell,' Prabu said. 'I love to laugh my asshole off.'

'Quite.' Thathi, wiping his cheeks, smiled. 'Man dies, goes to hell. He passes a shit-pit dug out for the British. Around it there are fifty armed guards. Dogs, barbed wire, a moat. The man asks the devil why so much security. Devil says these bastard Brits always try to escape. He passes the Japanese pit, and it's the same. Even more guards because they say the Japs have developed a system where they all work in tandem to get each other out, like a factory floor. The man passes the Sri Lankan pit, and there are absolutely no guards around it. You know why?'

'Very honest people?' Prabu asked.

Thathi laughed. 'No. The man asks why. Devil says he loves the Sri Lankans. Those buggers, ha ha. If someone is close to getting out of hell, the others drag him back in.'

TWELVE

You hold a meat cleaver in your right hand. It has dark red stains on it. You hope it's the blood of meat. Of animal, not human.

By your side, two other boys, roughly the same age, sent ahead with you to cut a path through the forest. To test for landmines.

You're thirsty, but you're sure as shit not going to ask for water. Licking the salty sweat off your arm. Holding your head up with your hands.

Bullets whizz off trees, shelling, explosions.

You know you have to get out of this.

I watch you as a sentry, still hopeful it's not too late. Still optimistic about what may become of you. Still believing you won't be scarred.

But I know I'm wrong. I can see in your eyes that it's over.

You're trying too hard. Up in the tree. Eyes locked on No Moustache Land, as they call it. Absolute stillness. Like guarding Buckingham Palace. Nothing can distract you. Not the smell of idli or pongal, not the sound of running tap water, not the noises of a cricket match below you.

Your gaze is locked. Too scared to make a mistake.

You don't even look down when you hear Tarzan's voice. When he wants to take you out of this place, he will. Until then, you can't screw up.

The cricket game happens every day, and after they finish, they challenge each other to hit the sentries. Tarzan lobs the ball up to all the Bronsons, who take broad swipes at it with the bat. Five metres below the sentry, in this case you.

The sentry's job? Don't flinch. You can get hit, but you must not fall out. You mustn't look at the ball until Tarzan shouts, 'Catch it.'

He's meant to do this when it's inches away and you trust him. Still do.

Every day, a sentry is punished for taking his eyes off No Moustache Land.

But not you. You're unbeaten, never flinch, never even bloody sweat.

You. The. Man. Even though you're really just a boy.

'Catch it,' Tarzan shouts. The leather ball's heading for your teeth. But you don't drop your gun. Don't drop your gaze, and when you're hit and the blood soaks your shirt, you don't wipe it away. You don't catch your falling tooth.

'Bravest kid I've ever seen,' Mr Majestyk says.

But they're wrong. You're friggin' terrified. Hate to be punished ever since Appa made you hold all your books above your head for two hours when you failed a test. You hate disappointing. Hate being shouted at.

Two weeks into your role and no one tries to hit you out of a tree with a cricket ball (unless as a party trick to scare a prisoner).

Two weeks into the role and Tarzan's still not so much as talked to you.

Then, I watch as they change their tune.

'Come play, kid,' Murphy's Law says. 'You can bat instead of Dirty Dozen.'

You point to your chest. 'Me, sir?'

'You.'

'But sir, will Dirty Dozen get—'

'Dozen's dead,' says Murphy's Law. 'Pad up.'

Mr Majestyk's bowling is crap. Balls that pitch too short, or too full. Cannon fodder, but you're scared to whack them. You know you'll get in trouble. But when you block three help-yourself-buffet balls in a row, Murphy's Law says, 'Hit the bloody thing or no dinner.'

You're hungry. Starving. Famished. So you pivot on your heel and hook the next ball for six.

'Shit, that's some bloody hand speed,' Murphy's Law says.

The next ball, you're on your knee, sweeping for six more.

Like a shadow looming, you can sense people moving towards the boundary. They want to catch a glimpse of this kid.

Next ball is the best shot yet, and these hardened

terrorists, freedom fighters, Panthers, whatever-they-call-themselves, are giggling like girl scouts, clapping, whistling, hooting.

And it's like this every day for at least two hours. I watch them watch you pulverizing whichever bowler they put in front of you each time you bat. Hell, they even kidnap the Tigers' fastest bowler to bowl at you and when you make a punk of him they kidnap the army's mystery spinner.

They can't get you out. No one can.

And now the Supreme Leader watches you. He's heard you're the best bloody sentry in Panther history and now they dream of you playing international cricket. For their homeland.

So you bow in front of the Supreme Leader after every two-hour knock and you kiss the guy's bearded toes, spitting out a curly hair each time. And the Supreme Leader tells you, 'One day, kid, I've got something very special for you.'

You smile. You dream. You think one of the most violent men in the world wants you to play cricket for Sri Lanka.

Still think it when the bowling machine is installed. Still think it when you're forced to read English books. Forced to learn the language.

'Kid needs more combat experience,' the Supreme Leader says. He beckons you over with his eyes, ties a cyanide capsule round your neck. 'You're special. They can never take you in alive. Never surrender. If they get you, bite this capsule.'

You're in the jungle. A friggin' jungle cat. Cradling an AK-47. No sweat on your palms. A raging fire in your belly.

Combat.

But as soon as you feel comfortable, you remember this is no game. No walk in the park. And you want to call out for Tarzan, for Appa, for Amma, for Akka, but no one gives a shit about you.

To your right, Mr Majestyk; to your left, Murphy's Law and Machine Gun Kelly. Puffing. Pissed off that they've been signed up to give you live combat training.

'Watch your step, little man,' Murphy's Law says. 'Supreme Leader will fry my cashews if you get hurt.'

'He's got something very special lined up for you,' says Mr Majestyk with a rapist's smile and a slap of the ass.

Ahead of the pack, two girls, aged twelve and fourteen. Their skin is fair for these parts. If not for the mud they would be almost, you know, burgher colour, and their skin would look soft. Their hair is the colour of dark chocolate, both wearing it in the same style. Tied into greasy plaits. Clearly sisters. The same leaning-back ears, the same protruding chins. The same slim noses and big eyes.

They're too weak to carry guns, but heavy enough to set off landmines if they step on them.

'Today, little man …' Machine Gun Kelly flaps his blubber lips, paints black stripes on his black face, like a black-on-black zebra. 'Today, little man, you kill your first Sinhalese scum.'

No one knows this except me, but you swallow your own vomit. No way, you think. No way. This can't be.

It's like a hunter's pack. The girls left out in the open as bait to draw out army soldiers.

You and the men lie on your tummies. Guns pointed. Fingers on triggers, but not yours. How can you kill a man? How can you kill anything?

No way.

The twelve-year-old girl collapses on her back. Sun's too strong. The men too scared to take water out to her.

'I can go,' you say, up on your feet.

'Down, you bastard,' says Murphy's Law, the sun shining off his bald head as he takes off his helmet. 'Not your job. Not your concern.'

The moon comes up, as do the stars. It's dark, and the men start snoring. The fourteen-year-old girl still on her feet.

You prod the three male bodies next to you. You tug at Murphy's Law's flask of water, but the strap of it is caught around his wrist. When you pull it, Murphy's Law mumbles something … Starts snoring again.

Training comes in. On your belly, you move like a snake across the dead leaves and broken twigs. Silent, stealthy.

'Have some,' you say to the girl.

She grabs the bottle, pours the water into the mouth of the twelve-year-old who glugs it between her grimaces.

'Raaga, my sister,' the fourteen-year-old says. 'They took us both, but they promised Appa they'd only take me.'

'Shhh.' You point to the men, then jump to your feet. Crouch, hop left and right. 'Shhh.' You look to the far side because you heard a twig snap over there. Could be animal. Could be man. Likely, if man, to be man with gun.

You pull the fourteen-year-old down, flat on the ground. Over her sister. 'Be quiet, girl.'

'Name's Tanaja.'

'Shhhh.'

This could be the moment. The time you're forced to kill in self-defence. You hear leaves rustling. It's happening. You slither ninety degrees away from the sound. Past the clearing, behind some kick-ass big trees, some out-of-control bushes.

The footsteps become faster, more distant, like a sprint.

'Catch him,' Mr Majestyk says from behind. 'Run, run, run.'

Gun held high above your head, you leap over a pit, dodge a bush, hurdle a branch. Now your gun on your back, pump those arms. Too scared to fail.

Bang. Shit. A blow to your nose, and now you're on your back. An army soldier above you, gun repositioned, cocked, about to fire, then a flashlight in your face.

Sinhala whispering.

'I no understand,' you say.

'How old are you, kid?' the soldier asks in English. He puts the flashlight on the ground so you can see his face. The soldier's handsome, cleanshaven, strong-jawed, skinny, maybe twenty-two or twenty-three years old.

'I have thirteen years,' you say.

The soldier lowers his gun, digs the butt into the mud. 'Too young. Too damn young.'

Squatting, the soldier pulls out a pistol, which he holds

in one hand, offering you water with the other. 'You shouldn't be fighting.'

That's for damn sure. Shouldn't be fighting; shouldn't have to prove yourself by killing a man. Especially not this handsome man who took pity on you.

Drinking your water, you eye the soldier's machine gun on the ground.

'I know you don't want to do that, kid,' the soldier says. 'You can trust me. I trust you.'

You can't remember what it feels like to be trusted. So you look at the gun again.

'I can take you home,' the soldier says. 'My name's Kusal. I can take you home. You like that?'

Wanting to smile, you shake your head. Maybe this is a test. Maybe the Bronson clan are watching.

'You hungry, kid?' Kusal pulls out a Kandos chocolate bar from his bag. 'I keep this for when I need to celebrate. Had nothing to celebrate in a year.' He breaks off a piece and gives it to you. Acts out chewing. 'Eat, eat.'

You can't resist. You shove the whole thing in your mouth. You reach out your hand.

Laughing, Kusal says, 'Like it?'

You nod, shovel another piece into your mouth, melted chocolate on your hands.

'Let's go home,' Kusal says. 'Bet your ammi and thathi want to know where you are.' He holsters his pistol, bends down to get his machine gun, which he straps to his back. 'Let's go.' He reaches a hand out to you.

You reach a hand out to your new friend.

But then your ears ring, and you can't hear anything,

and you feel liquid on your face, and your eyes are blurry, so you close them.

When you open them you see Mr Majestyk, standing above you, gun pointed at Kusal's limp body.

Kusal's head looks like a hacked-open coconut, and his blood is dripping off your nose. Your lips. Through your teeth.

THIRTEEN

Ammi served the boys food at four in the morning. Thathi sat at one end of the table. Prabu sat at the other, the length of a swimming pool away. Ammi and Indika on either side.

Prabu wanted to eat with his hands, but the others used knives and forks. So he picked up his cutlery with an overhand grip, stabbing into the kiri bath.

'Careful, Prabu,' Ammi said. 'I put too much chilli powder in the lunimiris. Ran out of onions. Very spicy.'

Prabu balanced a little kiri bath and a lot of lunimiris on his knife, dropping most of it into his mouth.

Sally ate what he spilt on the floor, flicking her tongue back and forth. She backed away and sneezed.

Thathi filled his glass with water. 'Maybe we should all eat with our hands, no? Easier to get the mix right. Tastier too. You like eating with your hands?'

'Do I?' Prabu asked.

'I can tell by the yellow on your fingers. The kaha, the turmeric in the gravy. Do you eat turmeric in your food?'

'I not so much sure.' Prabu finished chewing. 'I just

86

take anything they give.' His stomach started to rumble. The better the food, the more this happened. 'Can I take a toilet please?'

After a successful combination of number one and number two in a marble bathroom, Prabu found Indika in the TV room.

The Jayanettis' TV was bigger than Prabu's richest cousin's front gate. Flat, across the wall like a poster of the president at his camp, it blasted out sounds through four speakers, each the approximate height and girth of Sri Lankan spin bowler Rangana Herath.

Prabu took off his shirt, copying Indika.

'Remember, dude,' Indika said. 'You don't have to do everything I do.'

'Thank a lots, brother.' Prabu rolled on to his stomach, a cushion under each of his arms.

Indika shook his head. 'Don't worry about the smell of your pits.'

'I don't follow,' said Prabu.

'Never mind.'

The boys sipped hot Milo and dipped into manioc crisps, watching what Indika called a 'camera copy' of *The A-Team*, the heads of audience members and their laughter included in the filming.

Indika fell asleep soon after the opening credits. He slept from 5 a.m. to 1.15 p.m., in which time Prabu watched *Star Wars*, *Return of the Jedi* and *The Empire Strikes Back*. Worried he would never get this opportunity again, he couldn't waste time sleeping.

Indika stirred, looked at Prabu, jumped to his feet. Laughing, said, 'Oh it's you. I'm not used to waking up next to boys.'

Prabu smiled and showed him the DVD covers of the films he'd watched. 'Brother. Thank a lots for this opportune.'

Lunch was black pork curry, dhal and thick bread, washed down with passionfruit cordial. Then it was garden time.

Looking up, Prabu stumbled over a tortoise. Then he saw the tree house, balanced in the branches of a banyan tree. It looked like a five-star-look-out-tower. To the right of it, the water of a swimming pool shone in the sun.

Indika ran to the rope ladder draped down the tree. 'Race you up.' He grinned all the way, even though his careless steps swung the ladder back and forth.

Prabu tried to sprint, but the pain in his ribs slowed him down. Leaping off the ground, he caught a branch above. Swinging his legs up, he hooked them around another branch. He reached out for the lower level of the tree house and pulled himself in.

Indika got to the top of the ladder. 'What the? How'd you get up here before me?'

'Branches, brother.' Prabu held his ribs. 'Much faster than ladder.'

'You're like Tarzan.'

Prabu grabbed Indika's arm, looked around. Whispered, 'Who told you about Tarzan?'

'What do you mean?'

'I never tell anyone about him, whatever they do to me.'

Indika, blood-flushed face, mocked a laugh. Looked like he was taking a dump (but wasn't). 'It's in books, films, cartoons.'

Prabu grabbed his own ears, leaned back, said, 'Really? Tarzan, lord of the jungle?'

Indika said, 'The apeman.'

'Yes. Tarzan Subramanian, landmine removal expert?'

Indika let out a small laugh. 'I think we may be talking about different people.'

'Tarzan I talk of is famous in my hometown. Climbs trees like a monkey who looks like a human but climbs like monkey.'

'Who looks human?'

'No.' Prabu tucked his legs together against his chest, looking away towards the swimming pool. 'Who the hell is that hot chickie putting a swim in her bra and panty?'

Indika jabbed a palm at Prabu's shoulder. 'That, my friend, is my big sister, and she's wearing a bikini not her bra and panty.'

Prabu's eyes bulged open as the girl pulled herself out of the pool. He jumped to his feet. Threw his arms behind his head as if about to take a football throw in. *Beauty, beauty, beauty.*

'Prabu, right?' she asked, climbing the ladder.

'How you are know this?' *Beauty, beauty.*

Looking at Indika, she put her palms out to the side.

'He wants to know how you knew his name.'

'I know everything about you. That you had a fight with Shock Ice, that you—'

'Wow. How. The. Hell. You. Are. Know?' Prabu asked.

'Facebook. It's all over Facebook. Great new player at school, thought Isabella snogged him, Shock Ice beat him up, and my brother did nothing to protect him.'

'The guys had guns,' Indika said.

'I am also join the Facebook. Maybe I'll pork you tonight.'

'Hope you mean poke.' She jabbed his shoulder. 'Everyone's calling you a hero. My brother a coward.'

'Hello,' Indika said. 'Guns.'

FOURTEEN

Prabu became invaluable to Indika.

Any time Indika wanted a drink, Prabu rocked up.

Any time he needed a gift delivered to a girl, Prabu rode a bike.

Anything.

'Take a picture of me in a fountain, flexing my muscles?'

'Sure, brother Indi.'

'Help me dye my hair?'

'Sure, brother Indi.'

Indika needed a cat to spread self-written rumours ... Prabu. Was. The. Man.

And so, Indika always called for him. Always asked him to be by his side.

Kind of like brothers. He even called Indika's sister Akki.

Prabu couldn't wait for his first day at Mother Nelson Mahatma International College. What an opportunity. Everything falling into place.

But it was still school holidays. Two weeks till the new term. Cricket matches still to be won.

Indika broke his finger climbing a tree. Trying to be like a monkey who looked like a human. Failing. Falling.

With no cricket for him, it was a good time for Ammi to take him to the UK to look around universities. To choose between Oxford and Cambridge.

Prabu had never seen a plane before. Not one without bombs anyway. So he went along for the ride to the airport.

The jeep stopped in a no-stopping zone. A cop blew his whistle continuously, like he'd never stop. Thathi gave the dude a hundred bucks and he stopped blowing that damn whistle.

In time for the goodbyes.

Since everyone Prabu cared about had left him without a word, he wasn't used to goodbyes.

So he just flopped his arms by his sides while Indika hugged him. Held him tight. 'Don't score so much that they forget who I am, okay?'

Prabu nodded his head. 'Okay.'

'Run my replacement out.' Indika smiled.

'Promise.'

Opening the boot, Indika sneaked a plastic bag out of the side pocket of his suitcase. 'For you, bro.'

'What's in the bag?' Ammi flicked her newly straightened hair behind her ears.

Indika ignored the question. Hugged Prabu again. Held his cheeks like he was the Godfather. 'Brother.'

Ammi handed Prabu another bag. 'There's instant noodles, powdered milk, protein powder and Snickers bars in there. Don't let yourself get stick-thin again.' She kissed him on the top of his head. 'Come stay with us next week okay?'

'I check with my diary.'

The Jayanettis laughed and took turns slapping Prabu on the back.

'Tell him,' Indika said.

'Tell him what?' Thathi asked.

'Tell me what?' Prabu asked.

'I don't know,' Thathi said.

Blood rushed to Prabu's face. Genuinely pissed off, he asked, 'Tell. Me. What?'

'Don't tease him,' Ammi said. 'Just tell him.'

'We've hired a tutor for you for the next ten days. Prepare you for school. Also have a tailor coming to your boarding house tomorrow to measure you for new uniforms. I don't like the idea of you wearing hand-me-downs. And some casual clothing.'

Prabu's eyes got even wider than normal. 'I love casual clothing. Thank a hell of a lots.'

He dropped to the floor, kissing the feet of Ammi, Thathi and even Indika, before standing upright like an army cadet. 'I love very much Jayanetti family.' He turned to Indika, 'Brother, please don't forget me, okay?'

'I'm only going for six days.'

Prabu held Indika's shoulders and shook him. 'Please, promise.'

Prabu dragged his feet up the cracked steps to his dormitory, where a creaky ceiling-fan deflected leaking water from broken pipes. In the few days that he hadn't been there, his bed had been slept on, maybe even used for something not appropriate for unmarried couples. Prabu lay down on the damp mattress, his elbow touching the cement floor. He slapped at two mosquitoes on his leg, then pulled up the half of a striped sheet that had been ripped off for him when he first arrived.

He would have called his mother on the way up if the payphone hadn't been damaged by rain and if he knew where she was. Instead, he had almost shared his good news about tailors and tutors with the other boarders. But before he could, they snatched away his noodles. Ate his Snickers. Drank his milk.

In the fading light of a candle, he opened the bag that Indika had left for him, inside which he found a torch, a magnifying glass and two thick magazines. He put his head under the sheet, switched the torch on and read a note stapled to the plastic bag. It said, 'Machan, this should keep you busy. Turn to pages 243-271 in the first catalogue and 354-368 in the second one. Enjoy.'

Prabu opened one of the catalogues, flicking through pages of men and women dressed in winter clothes. He got to page 243 and stuck his tongue out. Two blondes and one African woman posed in their underpants. Through these underpants—some nipple. Some ass. The blondes and the African lady. Pretty much buck naked.

He pulled out the magnifying glass, closed his eyes. Kissed thin air.

Prabu awoke the next morning, thrilled that he had not opened the second catalogue. Untold treasures awaited him for whenever he needed a boost. He wrapped the two magazines up in the plastic bag, pulled the drawstring out of his cricket whites, tied up the bag and hung it out of the open slot in which an air conditioner must have once been mounted. He looked around, picked up Indika's hand-me-down coffin of cricket equipment, and left for the biggest match of the season.

For the first time since Prabu had joined the team, the Mother Nelson Mahatma International College Under-seventeens had bowled well, and even without Indika, Prabu believed that a target of 110 in thirty overs was a 'piece of piss' as Thathi would have said.

As unfamiliar as it was walking out to bat with someone other than Indika, Prabu pumped out his chest. Kept his chin high. After all, he had scores in excess of seventy in each of the four innings he had played for the team at the back-end of the season. If they could reach the target in less than twenty-seven overs, they would be through to the quarter finals.

The plan was simple: knock off the runs in ten overs. Text Indika the news before he woke up.

The close-in fielders of Mudalali International School greeted Prabu with Sinhala swear words. As with all the other teams, they hadn't done their homework. Sledging was wasted on Prabu. He'd heard worse.

He faced up to his first ball, which was dug in short. He swivelled on to the back foot to hook it over the short leg fielder for four. The next ball pitched full and he pressed forward, elbow high, and cover-drove it to the boundary.

The third ball landed short and wide of off-stump. Prabu threw everything he had at it, almost falling over. Counting himself fortunate not to get any bat on it, he took a deep breath, realized how close it was and knew that, without Indika there, it really was up to him to bat to the end.

Be tough. Prabu talked to himself as the bowler ran in. *You're better than them. Much more better.*

He danced down the pitch, his feet crossing over each other, lifted his head. Took a huge cross-batted swipe at the ball.

The fielders of Mudalali International squealed around him, until the ball dropped into the hands of the long-off fielder, who threw it back up in the air.

Prabu lowered the peak of his helmet to hide his face. Left the pitch, dragging his bat behind him.

Coach Silva rubbed his rice-belly and spat out the red juice of the betel he chewed. As Prabu passed him he said, for all to hear, 'You Tamil bastard.'

At the fall of the ninth wicket, Coach Silva locked himself in the players' dressing room. The last wicket fell in the twenty-second over with twelve runs still needed. Mother Nelson Mahatma's run ended. Coach Silva refused to come out to shake hands with his own players or the opposition.

Prabu knew he couldn't dodge the bullet on this one. After knocking on the dressing room door for over ten minutes, he was finally let in by Coach Silva, who then locked the door again. The stench of alcohol, vomit and smoke competed with that of the players' sweaty clothes.

Coach Silva, tears running down his puffed-out cheeks,

put his arms around Prabu. 'Why, boy? Why? Could have been the best day of my life. Made it the worst.' He released Prabu and thumped him on the chest.

Prabu fell on to a three-legged bench before springing back on to his feet. 'Sorry, sir.'

'I never expected any more of you Tamil bastards. You sabotaged me, I know.'

'Sir, I—'

'Shut up. You're one up on me today. You won. But I swear on my life, if we don't, if we don't win the next game, I kill you. Simple as that. Kill you, kill you, kill you.' He smiled, arms out by his fat sides. 'Who will miss another bloody Tamil boy? Certainly not your father.'

Prabu bowed his head, covering his teary eyes with his hands. 'My father is—'

'I know you made me lose. That's what you Tamils in Colombo want. Be part of us then make us lose. Make us smile. Make us cry. Make us look foolish to the outside world. We'll never give you your own bloody land, so you want to contaminate ours.'

'Tried my best, I can promise.'

Coach Silva pointed a finger at Prabu, showing off a new gold watch, which caught the only light from outside.

'You're much better than anyone else playing. I know if you want to win, we win. Next term is another league. We win. Swear on everything, we don't … Remember, I am the only one who doesn't believe your crap. I know who you are and which camp you came from. Not a bloody IDP.' He hugged Prabu again, slapping him on the backside. 'Now get out before I scar you permanently.'

Five days and four hours until Indika and Ammi got back. The only things Prabu had to look forward to were the catalogues. After the day he'd had, it was time to open the second one.

He ran up the stairs, peeked out of the open slot. He pulled up the bag and fell back on to his mattress.

Tugging the sheet over his head, he switched on the torch. Grabbing the second of the catalogues, he turned to pages 354-368, but they had other pictures glued over them. Pictures that showed severed heads of female Tamil Tiger suicide bombers.

Surely Indika couldn't have done this. Please no, Prabu thought. He flicked open the catalogue he had seen the night before. The lingerie pages had been ripped out, replaced by the picture he had seen in *Black July*. The one of the naked Tamil man at a bus stop, his head in his hands, as laughing Sinhalese men danced around him.

Prabu threw off the sheet just as a light came on. Four boys and the landlord of the boarding house looked on, giggling like gossiping bitches. Prabu grabbed at his bat, prepared to do some serious damage, but he knew he had to be better than that.

He heard choppers in his head. Gunfire. Water up his nose. Tasted blood in his teeth.

All imagined. All had to be blocked out.

Prabu's father had always said, without forgiveness there will be no future. Pushing past the other boarders, he leapt down the stairs, out into a storm. Sprinted along the potholed road.

The thunder drowned out his shouts for his mother. The rain engulfed his tears.

His phone beeped.

A text message from Indika in England: 'How, machan? Met Isabella and we're going to the cinema. She asked how you are. How are you?'

Prabu replied. 'I am jolly good, my brother. All is happy here. Please give my gentle greeting to Isabella. Miss you brother. Smiley face.'

He lay down on his back, his arms and legs in the air like a stranded cockroach. Rain pounded into him, and Prabu howled at a moon he couldn't see behind the clouds.

FIFTEEN

I watch you being woken up with all the other kids. The adults frantic, loading guns, packing trucks, burying evidence.

'They're advancing on us,' Tarzan says. 'Never expected them to go this far.'

You don't know how far he means. Don't know what he's talking about.

Somehow I do, but I can't tell you. Even though I try.

The Panthers had set up base between a school and a hospital. They thought they were safe. Thought that no one would shell the area because they may kill the kids, the doctors, the patients.

The Supreme Leader addresses the Bronson brigade. The kids' brigade, named Death Wish, looks on.

'The army has shelled our hospital. Our school. They're claiming it was infighting among our different factions, but that's horseshit. Buffalo crap. They killed our kids, and when I say our kids, I mean our kids. Mr Majestyk's son killed. Aged twelve.'

You kids gasp, not for a moment wondering why this

twelve-year-old got to go to school while you had to fight.

'My fourteen-year-old nephew, dead. Killed. Bombed,' the Supreme Leader says. 'I will not rest till I have ripped the hearts out of their kids. Given them a taste of how it feels.'

He lifts his machine gun above his head and fires, shells flying around him. The Bronson brigade all follow suit.

'Let them know we're alive,' the Supreme Leader says. 'That we're coming after their kids.' He looks down at you. 'We have a special plan.'

I watch them move base. I see them dig a new bunker for the Supreme Leader while the rest of them sleep on fallen leaves. I see them set up the bowling machine, feed you, make you do weights, read books.

I see them send you out on more combat missions. Somehow, you never meet with fire.

'We have something special planned for you,' Murphy's Law says.

Mr Majestyk interrupts your batting session for the first time ever. 'Come here, kid, come here.' He's smiling so widely his moustache is like a threaded eyebrow.

You drop your bat. Run to him.

'Wait here,' Mr Majestyk says.

Murphy's Law drives the truck up to you and Machine Gun Kelly flicks down the back panel, rolling out a dying soldier.

The man lands with a thud, coughs blood. Grabs at a hole in his abdomen, blood gushing through his hands.

'Sinhalese bugger,' Murphy's Law says. 'Want to kill him?'

You turn your back to them. Amble away, not saying a word.

'You jack bloody asshole,' Murphy's Law says. 'Not a party invite.'

Turning, you say, 'I'll fight the cause in other ways. Can't kill.'

'If you can't kill, you can't take on the special mission. The special mission devised by the Supreme Leader. That what you want?'

'I can't kill.'

Bullets rumble in the mud around your feet.

The Supreme Leader curls one end of his moustache around a finger, passes his pistol to Murphy's Law, marches to you.

'Son,' he says. 'This is your moment. The bastard's as good as dead anyway. Stick a bullet through his head, ease his suffering. He won't make it. You can take pity on him. See what it feels like to take the life of someone who may have killed your appa, your amma.'

He snaps his fingers and Murphy's Law jams the Supreme Leader's pistol into your hand.

Your fingers curl around it. No sweat.

I want to tell you, pull the bloody trigger. This man's as good as dead. You don't do it and then you're dead and so am I. I want to shout, pull the bloody trigger.

And I can see you take aim. Grit your teeth. Gun now to your own head. You close your eyes. I see you crash to the ground, head in hands.

Blubbering, the gun on the floor by your side. 'I'll kill myself before I kill another man. Another human.'

The Supreme Leader shouts, 'Get the bloody gun.'

Murphy's Law is there first, kicking away the pistol. 'Tie him up.'

They grab you by your arms and legs, stretching you. They rip off your clothes, cuff your wrists around a pillar, out in the sun.

Then they move on. Sit down for lunch. Have a drink, a smoke, a friggin' dance.

In front of you. In front of the Sinhalese soldier. Blood drying with the sand into a paste.

He is grunting. Chanting like a Buddhist monk. Crying.

And you feel like you have his blood in your nose. In your mouth. Between your teeth.

Your eyes lock on the soldier as his life lifts up out of him.

A day after he dies, flies around his body, in his wounds.

When it's dark and Raaga is on sentry duty, Tanaja, her fourteen-year-old sister, brings you some water.

You have to curl up your body to hide your nudity. 'Go, go,' you say. 'Thanks.'

When you hit cricket balls the next day, you ignore technique. Swinging wildly, nothing comes off the middle of the bat. All inside edges. But you don't care.

And I don't care. I've given up now. After what I've seen.

But you will try to block it out. Try to block the memories like you're blocking the cricket balls from hitting your stumps.

Everywhere you walk, you hear murmuring. People watching you, writing on charts, like you're an experiment. Jabbing your abs, pinching skinfolds.

They give you more meat to eat, always make sure you're hydrated, teach you basic maths, basic English.

No jaggery, they say. No rice.

And they make you sprint, do weights, climb trees and hit thousands of cricket balls.

They make you brush your friggin' teeth. 'Bad teeth don't fit in down there,' they say.

Tarzan Subramanium speaks of himself as a landmine removal expert, but really he's the master of explosives. He takes you away to a location so secret he struggles to find it. You wonder, in your own joy, if he is taking you away. Hiding you from the Panthers.

Instructed to cut through a mushroom-shaped bush, you hack your way to the 'pit'. This is a twelve-foot hole with the bush and trees as a canopy. It is furnished with legless planter's chairs, coverless sofas and plastic sheets.

Tarzan gives you a hoe, points to a spot, tells you to dig. It takes two and a half hours, in which time Tarzan smokes a pack of Benson and Hedges.

At the bottom of the hole is a metal box.

Out of that box Tarzan pulls six sticks of dynamite.

'The beginning of your course,' Tarzan says. 'Introduction to doing serious bodily harm with explosives.'

The course lasts a week, and now you understand why Tarzan is missing an index finger.

'You're almost ready,' the Supreme Leader says. 'Are you ready to kill?'

You remain silent.

The Supreme Leader laughs. 'Your idealism will be sucked out of you soon. In the meantime, we need to get you into a Colombo school. The kid from the north who can play for Sri Lanka.'

'Me, sir?' you ask.

'You, sir,' the Supreme Leader says. 'You need more training, more experience, but soon. How soon?'

'I'm working on it,' says Mr Majestyk. 'Will take time. Need report cards, scorecards, ID, newspaper cuttings. We're creating a new kid here.'

'Don't rush it,' says the Supreme Leader. 'We've invested too much. This is too bloody important.'

'Sir, you want me to go to school with the Sinhalese?' you ask.

The Supreme Leader's moustache bounces as he giggles. 'Your face says that you will be disgusted to do so.'

'They hate our people,' you say.

'And they will hate you.' The Supreme Leader chucks a cricket ball to you. 'Until they see you play.'

SIXTEEN

Indika scored ninety-four in the first game of the league season. Prabu only twelve.

This kind of pleased Prabu. Indi, his brother, needed the credit. Credit he deserved.

Thathi waited in the jeep for the boys. Didn't say anything when they shut the doors.

Didn't answer questions. Didn't smile. Just drove.

Twenty minutes, at least, till, 'Putha, you're really disappointing me.'

Indika winked and said, 'Good one, Thathi. Can't wait for dinner.'

'What kind of a stupid shot was that?'

Indika jutted his chin out. His chin saying 'whatever'. 'You do realize we needed ten runs to win. Seven wickets in hand? I took a chance.'

'And missed a hundred. I know you played well, but you should realize how much a hundred would mean to you.'

'To you, you mean,' Indika said.

'And your mother.'

'Not enough that they named me man of the match?'

'This is schoolboy cricket,' Thathi said. 'You should have higher aspirations. I'd expect you to be man of the match every bloody time.'

Prabu coughed.

'Unless Prabu is,' Thathi said. 'I don't want to be hard on you, but I tell my friends how good you are, and I need scores to back it up.'

'Ninety-four isn't a score?'

'Look, *Hi Magazine* wants to do a feature on you and—'

'I'd hate that because—'

'Putha, please. That's Ammi's bible.' Thathi pulled out his wallet and passed Indika a thousand-rupee note. 'Driver Ranjith's coming in the Land Rover. He'll take you boys out for some ice cream or something. Celebrate the win, but don't be satisfied. And, no, ninety-four is not good enough.'

Indika gazed out of the Land Rover window. Grunted one-word answers to most of Prabu's questions.

When driver Ranjith stopped outside the boarding house, Prabu asked, 'What time you pick me?'

'What for, dude?' Indika asked.

'The wonk.'

'The wonk?'

'Dinner tonight at the wonk for the anniversary of your mother and also your father.'

'The Wok, machan, not the wonk. I think it's just a family dinner, dude.'

'Oh, but I thought …'

'I'll pick you up tomorrow for school maybe?'

Prabu remembered Thathi and Ammi suggesting that he should come. But if Indika didn't think of him as a family member, what to do?

By the time he got up to his dorm room and looked out the cracked window, the Land Rover still hadn't moved. In fact, driver Ranjith huffed his way on to the pavement and signalled for Prabu to come down.

Prabu started to breathe heavily, worrying that something had happened to Indika.

When Prabu got to the jeep, Indika rolled down his window, said, 'Get in, brother. You're part of the family. Dinner wouldn't be dinner without your bloody goofy ass-face there.'

'Wow, wow, wow,' Prabu said, pulling a piece of paper out of his pocket. 'I have some good plans for surprise the Ammi and the Thathi.'

Indika laughed. 'It's not a surprise, machan. They made the decision, the booking, and they'll pay. Get in the jeep.'

'I need to get my party shirt.'

'I'll lend you something. Get in or we'll be late.'

Prabu clambered into the jeep, yet to take a proper breath. 'I also have two movie shows I buy for them to watch with us after dinner.'

'After dinner, I think they'd want to be alone.'

'You sure? I got a film with Antonio Boogaderas.' Prabu swung an imaginary sword before driver Ranjith swatted his arm away.

'Quite sure.'

'I have save some money,' Prabu said, 'so let me buy the dinner bill tonight.'

'It could be about fifteen thousand.'

'Shit the pants. Okay, maybe I let your parents pay. I have amazing present for them. I buy it from the fancy goods shop in Pelawatte.' He smiled, described it with his hands. 'A lamp shaped like a dolphin. Please let me get said items and come. It will make you amaze. Even though it have the appear of a dolphin, it light up like a lamp.'

At the Hilton Wok, Ammi, Thathi, Prabu, Indika and Akki sat around a table with a Lazy Susan in the middle. A waitress, in a high Chinese-collar dress, took their orders while a waiter poured green tea from a teapot with a three-foot spout.

After the staff retreated, Prabu, wearing a pink Ralph Lauren shirt Indika had lent him, pressed his hair down into a neat side-parting, folded his napkin and placed it back on the table. He cupped his hand over Indika's ear. 'Get ready to P.A.R.T.Y.'

Indika signalled to the waiter to play the CD he had given him.

Prabu stood up and clapped along as his feet moved from side to side, almost in rhythm with the background beat.

He looked around the restaurant. Everyone there seemed to be getting into the spirit of things. Lots of people smiled, some even laughed. Akki shook her head and mouthed something at Indika, raising her hands as if to strangle him.

Continuing to clap his hands, Prabu started his rap, no less.

I am a rapper, here to make a party.
Celebrate and congratulate,
Don't be late.
Don't hate.
Dance.
Dance.
Love you, Ammi.
Love you, Tha.
Your marriage will go far.
Love you, Tha.
Love you, Ammi.
This Chinese food is yummy.

The chorus of a famous song. Prabu mouthed along to it. Shook his legs, moonwalked, Indian dance, changing lightbulbs, stacking shelves, moonwalk. The WAVE.

Twenty years, they been an item.
There's no way to fight 'em.
Item.
Fight 'em.
Tall and strong,
Never wrong,
Ammi, Ammi.
Tha, Tha.
Love you, Ammi.
Love you, Tha.
You have a nice car.
Love you, Tha.
Love you, Ammi.

Very flat tummy.
Very flat tummy.

'Sing,' Prabu said. 'Like you promise, please sing.'

Filming everything with his phone, Indika shook the screen because he was laughing so much. 'It's too good for me.'

Thathi and Ammi leaned back in their chairs, smiling so much they had tears in their eyes. Akki buried her head in her hands under the table.

The music continued playing, Prabu obliging Indika's suggestions to continue dancing.

A group of young partygoers, dressed to kill, hooted and cheered. Prabu even thought he detected a reaction from the old ladies Thathi said were hanging on to their society magazine past, but it was difficult to tell as their faces looked to be pinned back in permanent frowns.

Prabu's gaze darted around the room. Like an opera singer taking in the applause. And as if as an encore:

Ammi and Tha,
Beauty couple.
The best beauty couple in the world.

The video of Prabu singing got 768 'likes' on Indika's Facebook page.

SEVENTEEN

Thathi slowed down near the school gate, blocked by a throng of girls. Pointing to the back seat. Pointing at Prabu.

Indika grabbed his hand. 'Wonder what's going on.'

The six members of the Scorpion Five approached the jeep, one opening Prabu's door, two others lifting him off his seat. Raising him on their shoulders, carrying him into the school, parading him around the basketball court.

The basketball court he felt he had seen before but had no idea how.

Prabu lapped it up. High-fived anyone tall enough to reach. Smiled so wide his tongue almost fell out through the gaps in his teeth. Rubbing his stomach, he made those whimpering noises he found hard to control.

Indika marched by his side, hands aloft, triumphant.

When the Scorpion Five lowered Prabu back to the ground, a girl threw her arms around him, kissing him at least twenty times, alternating cheeks.

Pulling out of the hug, Prabu got a good look at her. She had her hair tied up in a bun, which drew attention to the sharp lines of her cheekbones and chin. Her eyebrows were as thin as Prabu's mother's moustache. He had seen more beautiful women, some with smaller noses, but there was something about her. Something powerful in her eyes.

'Let the lord welcome you.' She raised her hands in prayer and chanted something.

'What she is saying?' Prabu asked. 'Is she speaking language from another country?'

'Tongues,' Indika said.

Prabu shook his head. 'No. Just on the cheeks, brother.'

'She's speaking in tongues.' He pulled Prabu's head towards his ear. 'That's Achala. Religious fanatic, but lovely girl. Most desired catch in school—'

'Most desired? Then she is tart?'

Indika laughed. 'No one's ever snogged her.'

Achala's prayer ended with an amen. She held a hand out to Prabu, blocking off Indika. 'You're the new boy, aren't you?'

'Eeeh heh heh,' Prabu said. That was all he could muster. Couldn't close his bloody mouth.

'I showed your video to the congregation,' Achala said.

'What video?'

'On Facebook and YouTube. You singing at the Wok. Rapping.'

Prabu looked up at the sun. *Oh shit where has gone my vision?* 'Ah,' he said, nodding his head. 'That is why these buggers who have carried me on their shoulders, sang same said song I sang last night.'

'You're a comedy genius, darling.'

Prabu let off a high-pitched giggle. Didn't stop for at

least thirty seconds. Being called darling by a hot girl may have been as far as he had ever been with one.

'What's the matter?' Achala asked.

Facing her again, Prabu said, 'Nothing, I just have happy. Not sure why this is as it is.'

'That's Daddy's way, darling. Daddy loves you.'

'I have not met your dada.'

Achala looked up, made a face as if blowing out a candle. 'Yes you have. My daddy is Jesus.'

'Wow,' Prabu said.

Principal Uncle limped to the assembly stage, resting his walking stick against the podium. He coughed, ran his hand over his grey comb-over and straightened his cravat.

Prabu thought Principal Uncle looked just like the men in those old English films he had watched with Thathi. Except that he was brown.

'Firstly I would like to welcome a new student,' Principal Uncle said. 'A lot of you will know him because he's been playing cricket for us. Potentially the finest cricketer we've ever had.'

Indika coughed in the audience.

'Apart from Indika, of course. Prabu, if you would like to come up onstage we can welcome you.'

Prabu. Prabu. Prabu.

Legend.

Master blaster.

Cheering, hooting. It felt familiar. Felt good.

After shaking Principal Uncle's hand, Prabu took the microphone from him.

'Indika is tell to me to go oral on stage,' Prabu said, reading from a sheet of paper. He had no idea why everyone was laughing. 'I am very excite to be here. Thank a lots for this opportune. I am of the name Prabu and I love cricket, athletics, reading books, and listen for the music. Thank a lots for your greet me.'

Prabu, chest out, strode back to his bench, winking at Indika on the way. Indika didn't wink back. He was too busy stopping his guts from falling out of his mouth.

'I am also delighted to announce,' Principal Uncle said, 'that Indika has been officially selected for the provisional thirty-man pool for the Under-seventeen Cricket World Cup.'

Indika stood up and waved his hand at all the people clapping, Prabu behind him, slapping his back.

The school building was shaped like a cube, painted in squares of red, yellow, green, blue and white.

'Looks like a Rubik's, no?' said Indika.

Prabu agreed, not knowing how he understood what this meant. No idea why the building looked so familiar.

Walking up to the fourth floor, Prabu jumped when he passed a monkey sitting on top of a storage cupboard, watching over the photocopier machine.

'Brother, brother,' he said, clutching at Indika's arm. 'It is monkey.'

'That's Suddha. Sweet fellow.'

'Suddha?' Prabu asked. 'You are know this monkey?'

'Named by Coach Silva. Because the monkey is always looking down on us like the white man. Like the Suddha.'

'How is that monkey get inside?' Prabu asked. He needed to know, for some reason.

'A trapdoor on the roof for the engineers to be able to access the satellite dish. It doesn't have a lock and Suddha knows how to open it.'

Prabu laughed, crouched, waved his arms.

'This is where the teachers photocopy and lock up exam papers. I've tried to bribe Suddha with bananas to steal them for me, but he wants nothing to do with exams as he's against animal testing.'

Economics was a blur.

Aggregate demand and supply, the multiplier effect. The balance of bloody payments.

Meant less than zero to Prabu. He nudged Indika, looking for explanations, but Indika seemed more interested in the lady teacher than in the subject.

When she had to go out to attend to a religious disagreement on the basketball court, she set the class a multiple-choice paper.

Indika didn't even turn his paper over. Instead, he wrote out a note, which he handed to Prabu to pass on to Tikiri, the class geek whose waist-length plaits left trails of coconut oil on the polished red floor.

She read the note straightaway, but didn't look around.

When the bell rang, Prabu leapt out of his seat and ran to the entrance of the library to see Achala.

Tikiri, head down, marched straight to Prabu. Slapped him so hard across the face that it made his spit fly, splattering the wall.

'I did not come to this school to have affairs,' Tikiri said.

Prabu held his face. 'I did not come here to be slapped.'

'You be careful of this boy,' Tikiri said to Achala, handing her the note.

One of the Scorpion Five grabbed it. Read it out.

Dear Tikiri,

When you scrunch up your dark face to read your notes you look so sexy. I love your thick eyebrows and the smell of coconut oil in your hair. I love how you wear your skirt up to your chest and how you wear long white socks. You are so hot, and I want you.

Love,

Prabu

Eruption of laughter. Even the EFL kids cracked up and they sure as shit wouldn't have understood the joke.

Prabu joined in until he saw the look in Achala's eyes.

She pulled Indika by his shirt, ripping off his prefect's badge. 'You're a disgrace. You're supposed to be looking after him.'

Prabu bent down to pick up the badge.

'No idea what you mean,' Indika said.

'Grow up,' Achala said. 'Find a new bloody game. You've been doing this note-writing gag to new students for four years now. It's stale.'

She slapped Prabu on the backside. 'Come on, let's go eat.'

Achala and Prabu sat under the shade of the ambarella tree, a straw each dipping into an open coconut shell.

'You've got to be your own man.' Achala locked her arm in his. 'Indika doesn't own you.'

'He love me very much. I am like brother.'

'But you have to tell him what you want sometimes, too. Have your own life.'

'I do,' Prabu said.

'Like, what're you doing Friday night?'

'Let me ask Indika,' Prabu said.

'Never mind what he's doing. Let's go to Lemon. Share a black pork curry and some mutton rice?'

'Is this what sometimes people call as a dating?'

Achala laughed. 'This is just two friends going out for a meal. Alone.'

'No Indika?'

'No Indika.' Achala kissed him on the cheek. 'Just you, me and Daddy Jesus.'

EIGHTEEN

'You know where we're going?' Indika asked.

Driver Ranjith, even though the jeep hit sixty kilometres per hour, turned around 130 degrees, grinned, his eyes shut. 'Of course, sir.'

Prabu sat between Indika and Gajen, the self-proclaimed leader of the Scorpion Five, a gang he called 'the most feared outfit in the Western Province'. Rajiv sat shotgun. He was the sixth member of the Scorpion Five, appointed thirty minutes after Gajen named the exclusive quintet.

The jeep stopped in front of the big Pizza Hut off Union Place. Driver Ranjith said, 'Sir, we here.'

Baffled, Prabu asked, 'Where are we?'

'Pizza Hut, sir,' driver Ranjith said.

'Why here?' Indika asked. 'Are we lost?'

'No, sir, you tell to me to bring you to Pizza Hut.'

'No, no, no.' Indika looked at his watch. 'I asked you to take us to P. Sara. As in P. Sara Stadium. Why would we have a cricket trial at Pizza Hut?'

'Ah.' An even bigger smile from Ranjith. Head wobbling, he said, 'You sure not Pizza Hut?'

Prabu said, 'Ranjith, you know where it is?'

'Of course I know.' Driver Ranjith got out of the jeep, strolled towards a row of trishaws.

Indika said to the others, 'He seemed sure when I asked him. Hard to read the bugger. Smiles if right, smiles if wrong, smiles if sad or happy, angry or calm.'

'Typical carefree Lankan bugger, no?' Rajiv said.

Ranjith came back to the car, tapped on the window till Indika rolled it down.

Prabu leaned back, away from a warm gush of air. Three trishaw drivers, in sarongs and open shirts, stood next to Ranjith, their smiles longer than their moustaches. Each of them put one hand on top of the car, above the open window. The sun peeked into the car through the hairs of the trishaw drivers' armpits.

Driver Ranjith asked, 'Where you want to go, sir?'

'I thought you knew how to get there,' Indika said.

'I do, but what is the name of the place?'

Prabu said, 'P. Sara Stadium.'

Driver Ranjith and the trishaw drivers cracked up, slapped each other on the back, spoke in Sinhala.

Driver Ranjith got back in the jeep, still beaming. 'Sir, you tell to me before to take you to Pissera Stadium.' He laughed so much he could have died. 'No such place.'

Indika huffed out a chuckle, turned to Prabu. 'Is there much difference in how I said it compared to how he did?'

'Brother, we going to get a late for the selector,' Prabu said.

'Can just say they closed the road for a minister to pass.'

'If session start late and finish late, maybe I become late for the Achala.'

Indika leaned over Prabu, said to Gajen, 'Tonight's his big date.'

'Not date. We meet for friendship.'

'No one is just friends with girls,' Rajiv said. 'Especially not one as hot as Achala.'

'I have many female friends,' Prabu said.

Gajen, squeezing his own doughnut cheeks, said, 'You leave it too long, she may look at you as a brother, then no kissy kissy.'

'She likes me I think, not like brother.'

Rajiv turned around in the front seat. 'Ask Indika. You don't make a move on a girl, she thinks you think she's ugly.'

'A dog,' said Gajen. 'Or they think you're gay.'

'I not a gay yet,' Prabu said.

'Well before you are,' Indika said, 'I agree with the boys. You have to make a move.'

'I don't think,' Prabu said.

'You're not interested?' Rajiv asked.

'Of course.' Prabu clasped his hands together. 'I like to make an affair with her one day, but—'

'But what?' Indika asked. 'Machan, you don't make a move soon, someone else may come along and get in there.'

'You told to me that she has not kiss anyone in school anyway.'

'Because she was waiting till she was old enough. Now she is. When you went to church with her, you told me there were lots of buggers who couldn't take their eyes off her. Those are your rivals. Jesus on their side.'

'Jesus,' Prabu said.

'You want me to come?' Indika asked.

Prabu rolled his head. 'She told to me to tell to you that maybe I should come alone. But maybe I have more confidence if you come.'

Driver Ranjith stopped the car at the entrance to a Food City and asked the security guard there for directions to P. Sara. Indika couldn't fault the security guard's smile, but he doubted the guard actually knew where the stadium was. All he did was point to the first turning.

'All these grounds have so many different names,' Indika said. 'Driver Ranjith, is P. Sara the one in Morotuwa?'

'Yes, sir.'

'Or is it the one in Borella?'

'Yes, sir.'

'Well, which one?' Indika got out of the car, made the kissing noise that meant 'could you please come here'. Five drivers came to the car. Then a sixth and a seventh. All smiled, all gave different directions with equal assurance.

Driver Ranjith started driving as if he knew where he was going, but stopped at a small kade—a street stall— built on squatted land, bang in the middle of a road. He got out to ask for directions again.

'He's wasting our time.' Indika pulled out his phone. 'Thathi told me I'd have to call him for directions. Annoying when he's right.'

At P. Sara Stadium, the boys dragged their cricket coffins behind them, jogged towards the nets where Coach Silva greeted them by spitting at Prabu's feet.

'You bloody bastards are late. You made me look like an idiot in front of the national selector. Indika, Rajiv, pad up.'

He held Gajen by the chin. 'Now you Tamil fools. You piss me off, you know? I give you Tamil boys a special chance and you take the piss. Gajen, you're not a good player. Not good enough. You piss off home.'

'But, sir, why did I get invited to this trial?'

'Not good enough to be late. Piss off.'

Coach Silva slapped Gajen on the back of the head. He tugged at Prabu's ear. 'Tomorrow, I will not sign your report card. You have three strikes before you get sent back to that place. Now you have one strike. One strike you're sure to get when you fail your exams. You stupid bastard. Maybe Indika made you late on purpose.'

A white man stood with a mounted video camera behind the bowler's arm. He loosened his old-school bow tie, diving after his straw hat when the wind knocked it off his head. It escaped him and jumped towards Prabu, who trapped it under his foot.

The white man tucked his shirt back into his Bermuda shorts, flicking sand off his knee-high striped socks. 'Thank you so much, young man,' he said when Prabu returned his hat to him. 'What's your name?'

'My name is called the Prabu.'

The white man's broad shoulders flexed up and down

as he laughed. 'The great Prabu Ramanathan. I've heard so much about you.' He reached his hand out. 'Steven Mathews.'

'Ah,' Prabu said. 'You are same Mathews who have play for England and have now a writer for the papers.'

Mathews nodded. 'You're one of the super little players I am here to observe. You and a ...' He looked down at his notepad.

'Must be the Papadum King?'

'Sorry?'

'Indika Jayanetti—'

'Ah yes,' said Mathews.

'He is the Papadum King,' Prabu said.

Mathews patted Prabu on the back and ruffled his hair. 'Well run along, your coach is calling. I'll keep an eye out for you.'

Prabu found Achala on the drinks balcony at Lemon Bar and Kitchen, overlooking the sports ground.

'Hi, babe.' She touched his collar with the tips of her fingers. 'Great shirt. The same one you were wearing in your YouTube video. Only real men wear pink.'

'That's what I told him,' Indika said. 'It's my shirt. Ralph Lauren.'

'Good for you,' Achala said, looking down her nose at him. 'Surprised to see you and Clare here.'

'Oh, was this a date?' Clare asked.

'Kind of,' Achala said.

'So sorry. We'll finish our drinks, okay, then go on somewhere else?'

Prabu smiled broadly and gave Indika the thumbs up.

Two hours later the four of them sat by the pool at Breeze Bar, on their second bottle of white wine. Indika turned towards Clare, placing a hand on her lap. She put her hand on top of his.

Prabu, sitting opposite, faced Achala and put a hand on her lap. She lifted it with one of hers and put it back on his thigh.

Indika lifted his hand and stroked it against Clare's neck, up against her ear and through her hair. He pulled her head towards his and locked his lips with hers. This was Prabu's time, his moment. His calling. Confident. Light-headed. Ready.

Wine was supposed to be weaker than arrack, but it made him braver.

He closed his eyes, put his hand up against Achala's neck and pulled her towards him, but she pushed him away, stood up and slapped him, making such a noise that Indika and Clare stopped kissing and looked up.

'Daddy's watching us,' Achala said.

'Shit, your father's here?' Indika asked.

'She mean Jesus.' Prabu turned to Achala. 'Why you hit me?'

'I'm not some foreign tart who kisses on the first date.'

'Did she just call me a tart?' Clare asked.

'I thought better of you, Prabu.' Achala ran along the

tiles of the poolside, slipping on some splashed water, falling on her ass. Prabu ran to help her up, but slipped and fell on his ass too, and by the time he was back on his feet, she was gone.

Another lost girl.

NINETEEN

'My name is Tajana,' the fourteen-year-old girl says. 'Remember?' She climbs the steps of the ladder behind the bowling machine. 'I will be feeding the balls into this thing today.'

Looking left to right, you put your bat under your arm and amble towards her. 'Should we be seen talking?'

Grinning, dimples on either cheek, Tajana flicks her hand to point you back to the batting crease. 'The Supreme Leader told me to.'

'Sure?'

'It's a nice change for me to get out of the tree.' She looks up. 'My sister. Raaga's her name. I told you that, I think. She's supposed to take my shift.'

A ball comes flying out of the machine. You drop to the floor to get under it. 'Hey, I wasn't ready.'

'You must always be ready.'

'Okay.' You get in your stance. 'Now.'

'The Supreme Leader thinks you're special. Has something in mind for you.

'So they keep telling me. Put a ball in, please.'

'But he says the school you're going to in Colombo will have girls in it.'

'Girls?' You stand upright. 'In a school with boys?'

Tajana tucks her head down towards her chest. 'You don't like girls?'

'Nothing like that,' you say. 'That's nice, but, I mean—'

'Just bat.'

Every day it's the same. Tajana feeds balls into the bowling machine and you bat. You try to teach her about cricket, but she doesn't listen.

Then, after cricket, it's lunch. A table laid out just for the two of you under a corrugated iron sheet balanced between the branches of two trees.

'No meat?' you ask Mr Majestyk.

'Running short of supplies. Bit trapped out here. Every bloody scout we send is getting killed.' Mr Majestyk ladles some slush into your metal bowl. 'We've all been eating this for months. Guess we're not special.' He rests the bowl on the table and ambles away, a joint hanging below his moustache.

You try to eat whatever the gunk is in your bowl, but it's a far cry from the beef curries you were getting. You want to talk to Tajana, but as always, you don't know how to start. You hope that she'll speak first, but she's silent. Looking at you from time to time, but turning away when your eyes lock.

'So your turn,' you say. 'Tell me about your family.'

'Father's a maths teacher. Mother's a nurse.'

'Where are they?' you ask.

'At home, I hope.' She looks around before whispering, 'They said they'd leave them alone if I came with them. Since they also took my sister, I think maybe my parents are okay.'

'As long as we do the right thing.'

'Always the right thing.'

'These schools, they have a dance called a ...' the Supreme Leader lifts his fingers, like bunny's ears, and says in English, 'Disco. Prom.'

'Boys and girls dance together?' you ask.

Mr Majestyk opens a file. 'The school we think you'll get put in, they call their dance ...' He laughs. 'They call it the Papadum.' He hands Prabu a photograph of a fair-skinned boy wearing a crown. 'This is the Papadum King. The most popular guy in school.'

'We want that to be you,' the Supreme Leader says. 'Then what you do will be an even bigger shock.'

'What will I do?' you ask.

'Later, later. Now we dance.'

'Sir, sir,' you say. 'Just one more thing. How do you know they'll send me to this school?'

The Supreme Leader holds his arms out so that he can be pulled out of his chair. 'You think we are stupid? This school offers a scholarship to a Tamil displaced person every year, normally for exceptional academics, but it can also be for amazing sports. No one can be as good as you.' He holds your hand. 'Now, my friend, let's dance.'

I see you asleep on your rattan mat. But you keep waking up because your stomach's empty. No more gourmet meat curries, just watery slush. But the funny thing you feel has more to do with love than a lack of food.

You roll over on your stomach and think you're dreaming.

'Shush,' says Tajana, her hand on your mouth. 'Don't say anything.'

'Are you crazy?' you ask.

'My sister overheard something while she was in the tree. Your mission at the school—'

'I can't breathe.'

Tajana moves her hand off your mouth. 'Do you have any idea what they want you to do?'

'Become very popular?' you ask.

Lying down on her side, Tajana whispers into your ear. 'They want you to blow it up.'

'Blow it how?'

'Blow it up, you idiot,' Tajana says. 'A bomb. They want you to kill all the kids there. Revenge for the attack on our school. Revenge for the Supreme Leader's nephew.'

'Can't be. They know I can't kill.' Shaking your head. 'And how could I ever get away with that?'

'That's the thing. They expect you to blow yourself up too. Become a martyr.'

You bolt upright, your lower lip out of control, your foot bouncing off the clay floor. 'I can't, I can't.'

'I know,' Tajana says. 'That's why we have to run away.'

'When?'

'Shush.' She holds a finger to her mouth. 'Leave that to me. One night. When my sister and I are on sentry duty together. Leave it to me.'

TWENTY

Prabu's poetry to Achala failed on two counts. One, it didn't rhyme, and two, she didn't read it.

His text messages remained unanswered.

Again, someone Prabu cared about had turned their back on him. Shunned him. Treated him like he was an unnecessary hassle.

Everyone did that. Except brother Indi.

It was Indika, after all, who gave him his latest idea, and it was Indika who dropped him off at Crescat Boulevard to put the plan into action.

And it was Indika who gave him the four thousand rupees he thought he needed to buy a silver pendant for Achala from the jewellery store.

The only problem was, the letter 'A' pendant cost six thousand rupees, but they had a discount on the letter 'I' pendants.

He deliberated for a while. Since Achala's name began with an 'A', the 'A' pendant might have been the more appropriate, but he knew he couldn't ask Indika, whose name began with an 'I', for more money.

So the 'I' would have to do.

The next stop was the t-shirt printing shop manned by one of the many girls in love with Indika, so Prabu was getting this free of charge.

Indika had written out the words for him to print: 'I score only for you, Achala.'

Now the big question was whether to change her name to Ichala on the t-shirt, so it matched the pendant.

He texted Indika to ask him.

The reply came in seconds. 'Are you bloody mad?'

Indika and Prabu rocked up to Henry Pedris grounds for inter-house football. The field, with all its random craters, resembled a warzone up north. More sand and mud than grass.

Prabu had never seen him play before, but he knew Indika was the school's star player. He didn't get the Papadum King title without being the best at most things.

Everyone Prabu knew had played cricket at some stage in their lives. Some too much for their own good, such as one-armed Aunty Lukshmee. Like most other people where he came from, Prabu had not played much football, but on the back of his prowess on the cricket pitch, Indika picked him for his house team. Representing Rambutan, they wore red. In their first match they were set to play Mango.

Achala sat in the crowd, under a Rambutan flag. She ignored all Prabu's attempts to attract her attention, either through design or because she was engrossed in her Bible comic book.

In an attempt to make his friend look good, Indika rejigged the team formation to get Prabu up front, on the last defender, ready for a tap-in goal.

The Rambutan house captain warned his players about Mango house's secret weapon—Christian, a ginger transfer student from Denmark. Indika assigned two of his biggest players to mark him.

At kick-off, Prabu tried to thread a speculative pass through to Indika, but instead placed the ball right at Christian's feet; in a flash of orange, he skipped over it, leaving Indika slide-tackling turf. Prabu helped Indika back on to his feet, just as the crowd roared, the ball bulging the back of Rambutan's net.

Kick-off number two, one nil down. Indika, from just outside his own box, marshalled his troops.

'Bong Hwa,' Indika called out to his Korean beast of a defender.

'Yes, skipper.'

'It's not the end of the world. Cheer up. You play sweeper, okay?' Indika clapped and called out, 'Gayan, you mark Christian also.'

Prabu shouted, 'Shall I mark Muslim?'

'No, no, stay on the last man,' Indika said.

'The Jew?'

'Christian's his name, Prabu, not his religion.'

Christian, with three men on him, was largely silent for the rest of the game, but the opposition Muslims looked hungry.

They were fasting.

From the kick-off for the second half, Indika took the ball out wide, used his pace and got behind the defence, dragging the keeper out of his box. He chipped over a pass, which lost pace as it arrived at Prabu's feet, behind all the defenders. Prabu trapped the ball with his left foot, turned to give himself a run up, and hammered his foot through the ball. But he hit the ground first. The ball bobbled up, at a very gentle pace, into the keeper's hands.

Prabu turned to see Indika holding his head in his hands, and in the crowd everyone was laughing apart from Achala, too busy with her Bible crossword.

Christian, at the other end, hit the bar with a scorcher of a shot, having evaded a challenge from Bong Hwa. From the resulting goal kick, Bong Hwa got the ball, drove through four challenges, lofting the ball into the box where Indika, arching his back, power-headed the ball into the top right-hand corner.

The Rambutan supporters went wild. Even Achala stood up to clap.

Despite the crowd's best efforts to make more of it, the game descended into a laborious affair in which neither side wanted to take a risk that could see them eliminated from the tournament. It looked destined for a penalty shoot-out until, in the last couple of minutes of extra time, Indika skipped through three tackles and found himself with a difficult angle near the goalposts. Prabu stood unmarked on the penalty spot.

Indika paused, having created enough time and space

for himself. Looked around, soaking in the chants of his name from the crowd: Indika, Indika, Indika.

His teammates started shouting at Prabu to stay onside.

Indika dropped his head as if he would power into the box himself, bluffed a shot with his right foot, and side-heeled a pass with his left into Prabu's path.

Prabu's first swipe at it chipped the ball up in the air, but he followed the ball, chesting it down, by accident, on to his right foot. Two metres out, he swung through the ball, banging it into the top left-hand corner with so much force the ball broke through the already damaged net.

The crowd remained silent. Since the ball rolled loose in the stands, there was uncertainty about the goal's validity.

All eyes on the referee. He whistled and pointed to the middle of the pitch. The Rambutans erupted. They charged on to the pitch to lift Prabu off his feet even though the match had not finished.

Soon after the restart, the referee blew his whistle for fulltime. Indika ran to Prabu, lifting him on to his shoulders, carrying him towards Achala.

'Now Prabu,' Indika said.

Lifting his Rambutan top, Prabu flashed his new white t-shirt, which said, 'I score only for you, Achala'.

Indika squatted down on the turf, allowing Prabu to ease off his shoulders.

Shaking her head, Achala smiled, looked down at her feet, entwined her fingers.

Indika passed Prabu a small box, which he opened while bowing his head. 'Small gift.'

'Oh darling,' she said. 'You got me an "A" for Achala.'

'Well, actually "A" was very expensive. The "I" was much cheaper.'

'But you got me the "A"?'

Achala placed the chain around her neck, the 'A' pendant against her chest.

Prabu looked at Indika, as he pulled the 'I' pendant from under his football top.

'I' for Indika.

'I' for Incredible.

TWENTY-ONE

The Island Nation Newspaper
Prabu and Indika Lead Mother Nelson Mahatma to Final Showdown

While they have never scaled the heights of Tendulkar and Kambli's ridiculous unbeaten 664-run schoolboy partnership, Indika Jayanetti and Prabu Ramanathan are making their own noises on the Sri Lankan schoolboy scene. Classmates at Mother Nelson Mahatma International College, Jayanetti plays the anchor role in their opening partnership, while the swashbuckling Ramanathan, with strokes Brian Lara would be proud of, has been destroying attacks around the island. In his eight games to date, he has scored 83, 12, 164*, 121, 176*, 49, 101 and a majestic 201*. His average is 184.2 and he has scored his runs at an astonishing rate. This newspaper is unable to verify the exact number of balls he has faced, but suffice it to say that all these runs came in a maximum of 30 overs. His opening partner, Jayanetti, has averaged over 70 in the same period, boasting a highest score of 94. His role has been to bat through the innings and he has remained

not out four times, which has boosted that average. The
pair has recorded century opening partnerships in all but
one of the games they have played this season. On the
back of this, MNM International is unbeaten, and would
have won every game, probably, if not for some dubious
scheduling during the monsoon which resulted in two of
their matches being washed out.

They face Catamaran International School in Negombo
on Saturday, in the final of the President's Cup. Their
opponents are also unbeaten so far, but their strength lies
in their bowling. Three of their spinners are in contention
for national age group honours. To add to the drama of
the occasion, the team for the Sri Lanka Under-seventeen
series against India will be finalized at the conclusion of
the match.

Prabu squatted, his backside just half an inch off the sand,
his arms hugging his burnt-matchstick-like legs. To his
right, a girl, maybe his age, likely Tamil, plaited hair and
frisky eyebrows, selling frangipani flowers to tourists.

When he smiled at her, his eyes and teeth resembled
camera flashes against his black skin.

'You come here often times?' he asked her.

Counting as she passed flowers from one basket to
another, head bowed, she paused. 'I work here every day.'

'Your smile is remind me of a smile I knew.' Prabu lifted
himself to sit on the side of a beach-docked catamaran.
He squeezed his foot between two wooden bars, posing
like a south Indian film star. 'You wish to make a walk
down the beach with me?'

'I don't even know you,' she said.

'In cricketing circles, I am called the master blaster, but you can just call me Prabu. Today we won big trophy.'

'I think maybe I have seen you in the newspapers,' she said. 'Are you also from Jaffna?'

'Near to there.'

'Can't even remember what it looks like,' she said.

'You can visit soon, I think.'

'That'll never happen. The Sinhalese see us there, they think we're Tigers.'

'That is easy to think, but you are wrong.' Prabu pointed towards Indika. 'He is my Sinhalese brother. I am the Tamil. Doesn't care.'

The girl dropped to her knees, placing the basket of flowers under the blue plastic sheeting. She dug the four corners of the cover into the sand as the wind blew loose strands of oily hair across her face.

'Let me help you,' Prabu said, pressing his palms against the side of the catamaran, trying to lift himself off it, but his foot jammed between the two bars. He looked away from the girl, shaking his foot enough to make matters worse.

The girl stared at Prabu, arms extended by her sides. 'I thought you were going to help me.'

Prabu rattled his foot once more, but he couldn't release it. 'You look like you can manage.'

'Typical man.' The girl bent to clear up. 'Leaving women to do all the work. What about that walk before my boss comes back?'

Prabu aborted his attempts to free his foot, instead

focusing on saving face. 'I feel a guilt to walk with you. I am loved by another female girl.'

'What? But—'

'Please.' Prabu lifted a finger to his lips. 'Say no more. Say no more.'

'It's just a walk and it was your idea,' she said. 'And who said anything about love?'

Indika jogged over, his hand shooting up to his mouth. 'You're stuck, aren't you?'

Prabu said, 'Don't be silly. I'm just chilly.'

'Chilling?' Indika asked.

'Yes,' Prabu said.

Indika looked at the girl and then back at Prabu. 'I'm sorry, have I just interrupted a Tamil Tiger child soldier reunion?' He started to laugh until the girl threw sand at his face. He closed his mouth a fraction too late, spitting out grains. 'Pass me your towel, machan.'

Prabu said, 'I'm stuck but—'

'I thought you were chilling,' the girl said.

Still bent over, slapping sand off his face, Indika glared at the girl. 'What's your bloody problem?'

She kicked more sand at him. 'You Sinhalese scum think we're all bloody terrorists.'

'I was just joking,' Indika said. 'We're all friends here. Just a bloody joke.'

'I told you what it's like,' the girl said to Prabu. 'He's your brother, is he? Don't take that shit from him. It's bad for all of us if you just take shit like this.'

'That is what my lady tells to me,' Prabu said. 'He is just putting a joke though.'

'Is it a joke that my father has to register with the police even though the war is over? Is it a joke that my relatives in Jaffna can't leave their house at night? Hell of a bloody joke, Prabu. Keep laughing.'

Indika grinned. 'Which question would you like me to answer first?'

'I'll rip your eyes out,' she said.

'Thanks. I wanted to keep my eyes out for girls anyway.'

The girl lunged towards him, raising her palm. 'You're a piece of shit. And Prabu, you're a bigger piece of shit for letting him treat you like this. Goodbye.'

'Tajana,' Prabu said as the girl walked away.

'Tajana?' She turned around. 'Who is Tajana?'

'Sorry I am mistake.' Prabu didn't know where that name came from. 'Never mind.'

The girl rubbed sand off her hands and marched towards the road.

Indika climbed on to the side of the catamaran.

'You think we Tamils are different?' Prabu asked.

'Rubbish, machan. Doesn't bother me.' Indika fiddled with Prabu's foot. 'Okay, lift your leg out now.'

Prabu did as told, jumped off the side of the catamaran. 'I saw you talking to that white sweaty again.'

'It's sweetie, not sweaty,' Indika said.

'Mad bugger you are for thinking any old lady will want action with sixteen-year-old boy.'

'Interesting you should say that.' Indika closed his eyes and raised a brow. 'She asked me to come to her room tonight.'

'No way.' Prabu jabbed at Indika's shoulder. 'Can't be.'

'Wait and see. Besides, at least I'm not pinning my hopes on snogging Achala. Until you grow a beard and walk on water, your mouth's going to be pretty lonely.'

'Grow a beard. Walk on water.' Prabu winked. 'Do you have a pen, brother?'

The thunder sounded like the bombs they claimed had stopped. Rain followed, thrashing down in spiralling sheets. A cloud of mosquitoes hovered above Indika's head, hiding from the evening storm.

Peering in through the window of Coach Silva's hotel room, Prabu kept his hand on his mouth to suppress possible laughter. Indika, meanwhile, used his iPhone to film the old bastard.

A bare lightbulb hung from a wire clipped to the ceiling. It cast a spotlight beam, cutting through the cigarette and mosquito-coil smoke, shining on Coach Silva as if he were a washed-up singer in an empty bar. He wore a jockstrap. That was it.

With his back to the boys, Coach Silva leaned forward on his right leg, bent at ninety degrees, rocking his bat forward, his left elbow high. The hairy flaps of his right buttock rolled over his crack like a gate to somewhere no one would ever want to go.

Tears rolling down the creases of his face, Coach Silva put down his bat, picked up a trophy and waved it at all four corners of his empty hotel room. Took questions from imaginary reporters.

'An honour for my goodself and my countrymen to lift this World Cup,' he said to no one. 'Did it for my great nation.'

Sri Lanka had won the World Cup fourteen years earlier, but everyone, Indika and Prabu included, knew that Coach Silva had blown his chance of playing in that tournament when he got drunk and bit the ass of an Australian player's wife. Back then he was thirty-six, an age at which you don't get second chances in international sport.

'I'll celebrate tonight by not drinking.' Coach Silva picked up a bottle, leaned his head back and poured some arrack into his mouth. 'I'll also kissy kissy my wife.'

'Keep filming.' Indika passed the phone to Prabu and knocked on the door.

'Who the hell is it?' Coach Silva straightened up, picking up a towel with which he tried to cover his jock-strapped genital pouch.

'Indika, sir. You asked to see me.'

The towel slipped out of Coach Silva's hand. 'Come in, boy.'

Prabu, out of sight, turned the camera on his coach; he staggered, his bloodshot eyes barely open, his man gadget edging out from under his jockstrap like a turtle's head.

Lifting up his chin, Coach Silva tried to bring his legs together, but his foot slipped on a banana leaf, some rice and a chicken bone; Prabu filmed the remnants of the lamprais, but ducked under the windowsill when he thought Coach Silva had seen him.

But he hadn't.

Instead, the crusty old bugger started laughing. High-pitched, pausing for life-saving breaths. 'Played well, boy.' He coughed up something he had to wipe off his hand. 'Your thathi will be proud. Good bloody fair Sinhalese boy. Future hero.'

'Thank you, sir.'

Coach Silva passed him a sealed bottle of arrack. 'Open the bloody bottle, drink.'

'Sir, you sure?'

'Drink goddamit. Don't coach you boys to be pussies.'

Indika winked at Prabu and the camera and pretended to drink without actually opening the bottle.

'Trophy we won yesterday,' Coach Silva said. 'I could be intimate with it. Could you?'

'Sir?'

Laughing again, Coach Silva forced himself to sit down. Head in hands, spitting, said, 'All night with this bloody trophy. Um yum. Sing it some love songs. English love songs. Sinhalese love songs. No sleep. Man, boy, whatever you are, one day you'll know what I mean. Feel the trophy, boy.'

Indika smiled at the camera. Exaggerated doing what Coach Silva told him to.

'Does it excite you?' Coach Silva asked.

Prabu thought this was no longer funny.

'My thathi will be proud we won, sir,' Indika said.

Coach Silva grabbed the towel and threw it over his lap. 'Your thathi is a good man. Always on my side. Big person now, but he's never forgotten me. I'm still his skipper. Tell the bugger your name has been confirmed in the final fourteen-man squad for the Sri Lanka Under-seventeens.'

Wide-eyed, grinning, Indika said, 'No way, sir. Does that mean …?'

'Means everything you want it to mean, boy. Come here. Help me out of this bloody chair.'

Stepping over two pairs of crusty underpants, Indika reached his arm out to Coach Silva, who grabbed it double-handed.

'Smooth skin, boy,' Coach Silva said. 'Your hands, not scaly like the other boys. Never done a hard day's work in your life, I bet.' He stood, one hand holding Indika's left arm, the other stroking his palm. 'Love these hands. Softer than my wife's. Boy like you plays cricket every day, still probably touched less balls than she has.'

Prabu caught Indika's gaze and signalled for him to get out of there. Coach Silva had crazy in his eyes.

'Sir, can I call my father?'

Head snapping up, Coach Silva said, 'Remember this day, boy. Anniversary of my star player's killing in the north.'

'Yes, sir. You told us yesterday.'

'Animals. Bloody animals. I need to speak to Prabu.'

'Sir, it's not his fault.'

'Know it's not his bloody fault. Still a chance for the bugger that we can mould him in Buddhist ways. Need to see him about cricket.'

'Good news for him too?'

'Don't ask questions. Send the bugger now.' Coach Silva lay down on his bed. 'Actually, make it tomorrow. I have dreams to enjoy. A trophy to caress.'

TWENTY-TWO

Tajana walks past you, doesn't say anything. Both of you look up at the tree where Raaga's on guard, her gaze locked on No Moustache Land.

When you're batting, you whistle to Tajana, who is manning the bowling machine. 'Tonight?'

She pretends to zip her mouth shut. 'I'll tell you, don't worry.'

'Tell me now,' you say. 'I need to—'

'Shussh.'

You stay awake as long as you can. Since you've had no warning from Tajana, you realize you should get some shut-eye. Rest for the big push, likely the next day.

So you float out of consciousness. Dream of cricket. Dream of bombs. Dream of children with blood all over them.

A jeep bounces along the path towards your rattan mat. The headlights dart, the horn beeps.

Lights burn around the camp.

The jeep brakes to a stop, inches from running you over.

Mr Majestyk gets out, falls to his knees. 'They killed them.'

'Killed who?' Murphy's Law asks.

'The army killed them. The army killed them.'

Pulling Mr Majestyk to his feet, the Supreme Leader, in just a pair of shorts, asks, 'Who, who, who?'

Murphy's Law is looking in the back of the jeep. Turns away. Retches. Cries.

'Who's dead?' You look up into the trees. There are no sentries. No Raaga. No Tanaja. 'Who did they kill?'

And you cry because you know.

Machine Gun Kelly holds you back. 'Don't look, boy. Don't look.'

But you're too strong. You elbow Machine Gun away. Elbow Murphy away. You see the plaits. The long hair. Covering their faces, but their bodies are barely dressed. Two young girls. Skin the colour of coffee ice cream. The dried blood on them like chocolate sauce.

Leaping into the back of the jeep. 'No. No. No.'

'They did this,' the Supreme Leader says.

'Killed girls,' Mr Majestyk says. 'Killed bloody kids. Animals.'

On your knees. Between their bodies. Stroking Tajana's hair. 'No, no, no.'

'They hate our kids,' Murphy's Law says.

It takes four men, grown men, to pull you, less than fifteen years of age, out of the back of the jeep. They hold you down on your back, pour water into your mouth.

'We have to tie him up,' the Supreme Leader says. 'God knows what he'll do.'

You can't close your eyes. A soldier now. On your back. Dry throat. Blood in your nose, between your friggin' teeth. Sinhalese blood. The blood of vengeance. You roar and it echoes through the forest.

You're at the bowling machine. Tarzan is feeding the balls. You hit them into No Moustache Land. Imagining they're Sinhalese testicles.

Clean strikes, off the middle of the bat. Focused. Brutal. Thinking of your mission.

The Supreme Leader was always right. They hate us. Don't even think we're human.. Want us all dead.

Let them see what it feels like.

But you can't help thinking. Why were the girls out in No Moustache Land in the first place? Why did they leave without you?

'Trying to escape,' Tarzan says.

'From us?' you ask.

'From war.' Tarzan increases the speed on the machine. 'Can't blame them, I guess. I've thought about it too.'

'You?' Bang. The ball hooked, travels for miles.

'After my son died. But I know I have a greater calling. Not fighting for me. Fighting for our people.'

'Our people.' Crunch. Like a bullet off the bat.

'What can we do?' Tarzan says. 'We have special skills. Can't waste them.'

You block the next ball so it drops at your feet. Picking

it up, you raise a palm out to Tarzan, who climbs down his ladder.

'How will I do it?' you ask.

'The war may end soon.' Tarzan hugs you. 'We could all be killed. Even you, though you're a kid. If it looks like they'll catch you, don't use the cyanide. Try to find a white flag.'

'But if they torture me?'

'Think of Tajana.' Tarzan's arm around your shoulder. 'Think what they did.'

'But—'

'You'll survive it. You have to.'

You're bowing at the feet of the Supreme Leader. The others look on. The camp is at a standstill.

'Now your name is Magnificent Seven,' he said.

'A Charles Bronson movie?'

'One of the best.' The Supreme Leader faces the crowd. 'The army is not worried about civilian deaths, so they will be here soon. Here to take us, to kill us, to rape us. So it is time, my friends, my people, that we burn the camp and we disperse. Move in groups of three.'

Murmurs in the crowd. Anger, twitching muscles.

The Supreme Leader signals for everyone to line up in front of him, and one by one he kisses every soldier he has, man, woman or child. And as they bid him farewell, they cry, ask whether he'll be okay.

'Just fine. They'll never catch me.'

They form another line. This time to kiss you. To kiss YOU.

'He will be our truest martyr,' the Supreme Leader says. 'A special child, he will become a special memory for our people.'

Loud cheers.

'He will avenge our mothers and fathers.'

Cheers.

'Our brothers and sisters.'

Louder cheers.

'Our children.' Cheers, maybe roars even. 'My nephew. Mr Majestyk's daughter.'

Chanting.

'And he will avenge Tajana and Raaga.'

You scream, nose scrunched up, gun firing in the air.

TWENTY-THREE

'Here, machan,' Indika said, passing a cigarette to Prabu as they stood on the main road outside their guesthouse.

Prabu removed the extra shirt he had worn to guard against the cool breeze of another flash storm. Now, as the air stood still and the water off the roads rose back into the atmosphere, he flicked sweat out of his nostrils.

The boys ambled up to a small shop and lit their cigarettes with the burning end of a rope hanging from the roof. Prabu tried to avoid the stares of the men eating rice and curry with their fingers by crossing the road. Indika pulled him back just in time to escape being flattened by one of the two honking buses racing each other to the next stop.

'You are,' Indika said, 'without doubt, the worst crosser of roads I have ever seen in my life. In a country where the people are world champions at walking in the middle of the road, this is quite some achievement. Like you're on a bloody suicide mission.'

Indika dragged Prabu up the road and behind the

sandbags of an unmanned military checkpoint. He unzipped the rucksack on Prabu's back, pulling out firecrackers, each one the size of a cricket ball, strung together like machine gun ammo.

Taking a deep drag of smoke into his lungs, Indika lit the firecracker wick with the red tip of his cigarette. Cracking up with laughter, the boys ran towards a low wall, which they jumped over.

They blocked their ears with their hands but could still hear the rat-a-tat-tat of the crackers going off, lighting up the checkpoint as if gunfire came from it. Bats, dropping from a tree above them, flapped their wings just before hitting the ground.

A silver Nissan March, headlights bouncing, brakes screeching, spun around 360 degrees before shooting off straight again in the direction of a palm tree, which bent over the car on impact.

Indika and Prabu ducked their heads below the wall, short of breath, no sign of laughter any more.

'Oh my bloody god,' Indika said. 'Quick, quick, run.'

Prabu held on to his upper arm. 'Brother, wait.' He pointed to the crashed car, its airbag deployed. 'Is the driver okay?'

Indika buried his head in his hands. 'We're dead.'

'What about the driver?'

'Come on,' Indika said. 'We have to get out of here.'

Prabu couldn't get his legs to work. Pictured dead bodies. Blood. All in his head.

The car door opened and a man pressed his hands against the airbag, pulling himself out. He walked to the front of the car to check the damage. A crowd of onlookers engulfed the accident site like zombies rising from their graves in a B-movie cemetery.

Prabu leapt up and turned towards the shop. A man, with specks of dhal on his fingers, turned a policeman to face the two boys.

Smooching noises, claps, high-pitched Sinhala voices, followed by the splatter made by Bata slippers against wet asphalt.

Prabu pulled at Indika's shirt. They clambered back over the wall, on to the main road, heads down, sprinting.

A man in a bunched-up sarong chased them on his bike. The boys zigzagged down the road, out of reach of the cyclist, who kept overshooting them and then doubling back.

Ahead, under one of the few streetlights that worked, a rotund policeman lifted a gun above his head. The boys ran down the driveway of the guesthouse neighbouring theirs, vaulting over a wall outside Coach Silva's room. They tiptoed past it, hunched, adrenaline pumping, and then crawled up the stairs as flashlights beamed around them.

Indika's hand shook so much he struggled to get the key in the lock of their room door.

Prabu felt at ease, but Indika wouldn't let go of the key. 'Break it down,' he said. 'They're coming up the stairs. Break it down.'

The heavy footsteps gained speed.

Prabu shoulder-barged the door, but nothing. 'Shall I kick it?'

'Too noisy.'

Prabu looked around. The only way down was via the stairs they had just come up. 'We are dead as two ducks.'

Indika held either side of Prabu's face. 'Don't tell the cops you're Tamil.'

A door opened at the end of the corridor. A white man in a batik dressing gown and long white socks, smoking a pipe, stuck his head out, put his finger to his lips and beckoned them over. 'Quick.'

They closed the door behind them, a second before the beam of a flashlight sneaked through the keyhole.

'Mathews sir?' Prabu asked.

He nodded. 'Shush.'

'You know him?' Indika asked.

The man outside knocked on Mathews' door.

'Get under the bedcovers,' he said to the boys. 'I'll deal with this.'

Steven Mathews opened the door, rubbing his eyes. 'What is it, officer?'

Prabu looked through a hole in the sheet when the light was switched on.

A policeman pushed his way into the room. Seemingly unperturbed by the night, he wore wraparound sunglasses which were too small for him, making the rest of his face bulge around them. He stood, hands on hips, his walkie-talkie making noises like a taxi radio. 'Are there people under those sheets?'

Mathews whispered, 'They locked themselves out of their room this evening, so I let them sleep here.'

'Been here all night?' The policeman asked.

'Since about eight.'

'Sure about that?'

He glared down at the policeman. 'Certain.'

'Where you from?'

'England.'

'Mr England man, you must be knowing how this looks. I was looking for boys who let off crackers and caused an accident, but I think I may have found something worse.'

'I do not appreciate what you're insinuating,' Mathews said.

'A man over sixty. A white man, a suddha, sharing a room with two teen boys.'

'Just helping them out. And I'm only fifty-five.'

'I am hoping that these are the boys who let off the crackers. I just wanted to lecture them. If they're not, you have a lot of questions to answer.' The policeman walked to the bed, pulled back the sheets, to find the two boys fully dressed.

'Lock the door, England man,' the policeman said, before turning back to the boys. 'Stand.' He looked Prabu up and down, scrunching his nose up at him. 'Tamil?'

'Yes, sir.'

'Papers?' the cop said.

'Sir, I think I am too young to be made to carry ID,' Prabu said.

'You're too Tamil not to.' The policeman turned back to Mathews. 'We have a problem here. A real problem. A suddha with a Tamil boy with no ID who just tried to bomb a checkpoint.'

'Bloody hell, it was just some crackers,' Indika said.

The policeman swung around and backhanded a slap across Indika's face.

Prabu raised his hand, but Indika held him back before the policeman noticed.

The cop said, 'When I need to speak to you, I will.'

'Can we talk outside?' Mathews asked, slinging a man-bag across his shoulders.

With the door shut, Indika and Prabu inched towards the window and watched Mathews count out some large notes, which he placed in the smiling policeman's hands.

He re-entered the room, locking the door behind him. 'All sorted.'

'How much did you have to give him, sir?' Indika asked. 'Looked a lot.'

'Just a little loose change.' Mathews sat back down in a chair. Poured himself a glass of vodka.

'If that's loose change, why are you staying in a place like this?'

'You ask a lot of questions.' Mathews laughed. 'This guesthouse was recommended by friends. Has a lot of charm. As long as you don't try to blow up a checkpoint, they seem to leave you pretty much to your own devices.'

'Brother, this is Steven Mathews.' Prabu's legs twitched as if he were about to jog on the spot. 'England opening batsman.'

'No way,' Indika said. 'What are you—'

'I'm here to watch you two play.'

Prabu said, 'But we—'

'Coach Silva will arrange it. A trial for you boys. But

I doubt he would have expected you to be up this late.'

'I guess we should be going to bed,' Indika said.

Mathews pointed towards the door. 'You guess right.'

'Don't tell to Coach Silva that you are see us, okay sir?' Prabu asked.

'So long, my friend, as you don't tell him you saw me.'

TWENTY-FOUR

Holding on to the rails as he inched down the stairs, Prabu looked at the two feet of muddy water in the guesthouse's swimming pool, which they had been promised would soon be in use. Since it wasn't, he tried to use the shower to wash the blackness of the asphalt from the night before off his feet, but it spluttered out rusty sludge.

He knocked on Coach Silva's door after the fourth chime of the bell from the cathedral down the road.

'Enter.'

'Hello.' Prabu tiptoed towards the trophy, clapping his hands together to kill a mosquito. 'Sir?'

Coach Silva lay on his bed, behind a cloud of smoke and a mosquito net. He sipped at a milky liquid in a plastic bottle. 'Want some toddy?' he asked, squeezing the bottle through a hole in the net.

'No thank you, sir.'

'Don't know how things work with you Tamils, but with my people, if offered something by an elder, rude not to take.'

Prabu grabbed the toddy bottle with both hands. He wiped its mouth on his shirt, closed his eyes and took a swig of the drink, spitting out a large red ant in the process.

'Forgot to tell you to watch out for insects,' Coach Silva said. 'Natural drink, sapped from palm trees. Filter the bugs through your teeth.'

Prabu took another sip of the thick white liquid. 'This is contain the alcohol?'

'Do popes shit in the woods?' Coach said. 'Or do I mean bears?'

'Something is in my throat, sir.' Prabu was taking in rapid breaths through his nose.

'Big boy now. Batted like a beauty yesterday. Deserve to celebrate. One day it will be champagne. Today, toddy.'

Coach Silva rose out of bed, his double chin inching into the natural light coming in through the glass door. He wore a blue-and-white batik sarong and a stained white vest, bunched up above his belly.

Prabu dropped to his knees and air-kissed Coach Silva's hairy feet.

'Best day of my life, Prabu,' Coach Silva said. 'Hero's welcome at the press conference this morning. Second year in charge of an international school team, win a bloody national trophy.' He lit a beedi. 'Tobacco wrapped in a tendu leaf. Want some?'

Prabu took a drag, holding the smoke in his mouth for a few moments, hoping it would relax him, but he released it all in one cough.

'Look around you, boy,' Coach Silva said. 'What do you see?'

'I don't know, sir. It is dark.'

Coach Silva shook his head and asked, 'Then what do you smell?'

'I smell, sir. Not sure. Um, the sea?'

'What else, boy?'

'The fish? My sweat? The smoke from backside of bus. My ...' Prabu closed his eyes, feeling like he was sitting for a test at school in a language he hadn't mastered.

'Smell your hands, boy,' Coach Silva said. 'Your palms are red-coloured.'

'Leather smell.'

'Is there blood on your Tamil hands?' Coach Silva asked.

'They're red-coloured from the cricket ball,' Prabu said.

'The smell in the air?'

Prabu breathed deeply through his nose. 'I don't know.'

'Gunpowder,' Coach said. 'I can smell burning, fire, bombs, bastard terrorists. The Panthers tried to stop us from becoming a great nation. You still support them?'

'No way.'

'Then learn the bloody language of our country. I can't speak your jungle Tamil, and why should I talk to you in the language of our colonial masters?'

'Sorry, sir. I will learn Sinhala.'

'Many hate your people,' Coach Silva said, 'so you need to work harder than the others. You have ten times more talent than Indika. He told you what I spoke to him about?'

'No, sir.'

'Bugger's been shortlisted for Sri Lanka Under-seventeen. Should be you. You're the great player in this team. Your name's on the tip of people's tongues, but because it's a Tamil name, only those with long tongues.' Coach Silva chuckled. 'Gave Indika's name because his father's connected. Want to give your name also. Would you like that?'

'Please, sir.'

'Have a problem, boy. Lost respect for you when you played that idiot shot yesterday. Doesn't matter how many runs you scored.'

'We won, sir.' It felt like the room was a boat, rocking on rough seas.

'Trained you hard. Taught you to be a man, but you played that bastard bitch shot. Trying to impress some sweet chick in the crowd?'

Prabu wiped sweat off his forehead. Looked down at Coach Silva's feet.

'Winning isn't the only thing. Other teams say I have a Tamil boy I can't control.' Coach Silva picked up the trophy, lifting it over his head. 'Winner of the championship mocked because he can't handle his bloody Tamil boy. You have to respect me. Have to respect the game. Why aren't you drinking?'

Prabu took another sip of toddy, remembering that Indika had played a silly shot too. 'Sorry, sir.'

'Want to respect you, but how?' Coach Silva asked. 'Can leave it like this. Or can punish you, and then maybe I'll forget this and respect you again. Maybe then I can sign your report card. What do you want, son?'

Prabu didn't have time to weigh his options. 'Sir can punish me. That can make it better?'

Coach Silva nodded and passed Prabu the bottle. He kicked away the dirty clothes on the floor, finding a wicker cane, which he slapped against his palm. As he pulled the curtain across the glass door, dust blew out over him. 'Bend over, son.'

'Sir, I thought—'

Coach Silva pushed Prabu's head down until it rested on a table.

The whistle of the first slash of the cane seemed to come long before the pain. The imported shorts Indika had let Prabu wear did little to cushion the blows. It felt like it did when he was stung by a jellyfish: a sharp, burning sensation. Prabu wrapped his lips around his teeth to keep himself from being too loud. Be strong, he thought. Be strong. An international cricketer doesn't cry after he gets a beating.

The cane dropped to the floor. 'Turn this way.' Coach Silva put his arms around Prabu, kissed his head. 'Sorry. Best way for you to learn.'

Prabu wiped his tears away on Coach Silva's vest, realizing this to be a mistake as soon as he had done so. Coach Silva's body stank of stale smoke and toddy sweat, urine and vomit.

'Hope that hurts and leaves a scar so that you can remember. In 2015, maybe you'll lift the World Cup. Can look at your scars and they'll remind you of your struggles to get there. Understand?'

'I do,' Prabu said, not believing himself for one second.

Coach Silva locked the bedroom door and picked up a torch. 'Let's look at your bruises.'

'Sir, they are below my shorts. Don't think you can see.'

Coach Silva snickered, lifted his shoulders and covered his face with his hands. 'You play international cricket, you'll have much harder things to do than pull your shorts down in front of your beloved coach. Only asking you to show me where it hurts. Scared?'

'I'm never scared, sir.' Prabu tried to hide how much his hands trembled as he pulled the elastic of his shorts down to expose his welts.

'Knew it would be hard to see bruises on your black skin.' Coach Silva bent down low enough for Prabu to be able to feel warm breath on his backside. 'Maybe better if I touch.'

'No, sir.' Prabu pulled up his shorts, turning around to face Coach Silva. 'Please don't. I beg you, sir, please don't.'

'Son, playing for the national side, boys will rag you. Must be prepared.'

'Please.' Prabu backed away towards the bathroom. 'I'll try much harder next time.'

Coach Silva giggled again. 'You're acting like a girl.'

'I'm not putting an act, sir. I'm begging.' Tears dripped down Prabu's face into his mouth. The room appeared to dance around him like the growing flames of a bush fire.

'Come on, baba. This is important for your development. Soon you'll be playing with men.'

'I'll quit cricket, sir.'

Coach Silva shook his head and said, 'Back in July 2009, two months after the war ended, someone invited me to a camp in the north. In this camp, former child soldiers were taught to play many sports. I taught them cricket.' Coach Silva grabbed Prabu's chin. 'You listening?'

'Yes, sir.'

'You know who was in charge of that camp?'

Prabu covered his eyes with his hands.

'The man in charge was a bugger by the name of Colonel Thisara. Can I ask you, were you ever at an IDP camp?'

'No, sir.'

'A rehabilitation camp?'

Prabu nodded.

'See, a white bugger like Carter wouldn't know the difference between an IDP camp and a rehab camp even if they had told him the truth. A stuck-up Sinhalese like Principal Uncle, born with a silver spoon in his fat asshole mouth, probably didn't take the time to look it up. Is there a difference?'

'Yes, sir.'

'You see, an IDP camp is for people who lost their homes, no? Like they think happened with you. But a rehabilitation camp is for former Panthers, no?'

'Sir, they make a mistake.'

Coach Silva laughed. 'All one big misunderstanding, no? So why don't your parents help?'

'I've misplaced them.'

'Your father took the babies delivered by the Panther bitches to the orphanage. And you helped him?'

'Never hurt anyone.'

'Then maybe your daddy was killed by the Panthers he

worked for, no? Your mother ran away with your sister, but she left you.'

Prabu fell to his knees, hands up in prayer. 'My sister got shrapnel. They allow my amma to take her to doctor.'

'But she left you?'

Prabu could barely breathe through his own howling. 'She had no choice.'

Grabbing Prabu by his collar, Coach Silva dragged him on to his feet. 'And you became a bloody Panther.'

Prabu didn't know the answer. Remained silent till he was punched in the gut.

'I read about child soldiers and their therapy. That after trauma they cannot trust people. They don't feel like they're trusted. They're socially backward, maybe mentally backward like you.'

'I'm not a soldier—'

'That they have anger issues. This is so?'

'Sir …'

'But if something bad happens, maybe the child soldier will remember the fighting, the death, the fact that he is a killer. And then the anger comes out—'

'I never kill—'

'The fact that he never had a childhood, that his friends were shot.' Coach Silva lit a cigar. 'So you're scared to go back to rehab camp?'

Prabu wiped his eyes, said, 'They were nice to me there. Colonel Thisara was nice to me.'

'So I'll recommend you get sent back.'

'Please, sir. I am happy here. I am very happy here, sir.'

Coach Silva giggled like a schoolgirl. 'What have you got to lose? Your boarding house?'

'Sir, my friends.'

'You think that Christian bitch wants to have an affair with a child soldier? You think the Jayanettis want a Panther staying in their house?'

Coughing, Prabu said, 'Sir, I am not Panther.'

'You think Indika will believe you?'

Prabu, looking down at Coach Silva's feet, shook his head.

'You won me my trophy. I like boys who win me trophies.'

'Please help for me, sir.'

Coach Silva smiled. 'What will you do for me if I do?'

'What do you want, sir?'

'I think you know what I want.'

Prabu clenched his teeth and growled. This was just like facing the fastest bowler around. That's what he had to think. No pain, no gain. That which doesn't kill you ...

Coach Silva put one hand around Prabu's throat and pressed into his Adam's apple. Prabu gagged on an empty breath and could feel blood flooding his head. He opened his mouth enough for Coach Silva to empty the remainder of an arrack bottle into it.

Prabu opened his eyes; his head pounded and his tongue felt like sandpaper against the inside of his mouth. Slime green and mustard yellow bathroom tiles surrounded him. The toilet was a squatting pan, crusty shit and thick piss around it.

A cockroach scurried over his feet as he brushed away a squadron of red ants that marched through the ridges of his abdominal muscles.

He looked out through a cracked window. On the beach across the road, a batsman top-edged a pull shot, lofting the ball miles in the air. Indika ran after it, his hair flapping in the wind, taking the catch over his shoulder, diving forward into the sea. His teammates whooped, buzzing around him like the mosquitoes that sucked at Prabu's ankles.

He closed his eyes again.

Coach Silva coughed. 'Kept me waiting a long time, boy.' He dragged Prabu into the bedroom. 'No fighting now.'

Prabu breathed in deeply through his nose and tried to make a dash for the door. But his legs failed him, taking him in directions he didn't mean to go. Stumbling. Drunk.

Without skipping a beat, Coach Silva threw him against a wall and dug his elbow into his spine.

'Heads, you try that again and I snip snip your dick. Tails, behave and play for Sri Lanka. What's it going to be, skipper?'

Prabu wanted to fight. Wanted to defend himself, but every moment that passed he felt weaker. His eyelids flickering, vision blurred. Unable to speak. The room swinging around him.

Lifting his sarong, Coach Silva tied it up again; he splashed talcum powder under his armpits and spat into his hands.

Prabu turned away to face the glass door and could

see through a sliver of a gap in the curtain. Outside, a white man. Steven Mathews, was it? Undoing his bow tie, knocking on doors around the pool.

Maybe this was a drunken hallucination.

'Help,' Prabu shouted, but with too much hesitancy and too little breath to be heard.

Coach Silva put a hand over Prabu's mouth. Looked over his shoulder and out through the gap in the curtain. 'You better keep your bloody machine gun Tamil mouth shut or you'll blow everything.'

Grabbing a tennis ball from his kit bag on the floor, Coach Silva squeezed it between his hairy hands, before wedging it into Prabu's mouth.

Prabu could feel the corners of his lips stretching open. He tried to scream but his whimper had no carry.

Coach Silva heard, though, and he responded by punching the tennis ball deeper into Prabu's mouth, making him gag. 'Don't try that shit, boy.'

Prabu looked through the curtain again. Saw Mathews coming closer. He knew that his only chance of being saved was to get the attention of his white knight. He pretended to trip, banging against the glass door; it didn't shatter, but it made a hollow noise like one beat of a drum.

Mathews turned towards the noise, took off his straw hat, and wiped raindrops off his thick glasses. He moved closer. 'Hello,' he said, banging on the locked door. 'Hello.'

'Keep quiet, boy,' Coach Silva said, switching off his torch and tucking his vest back into his sarong. 'Make any noise and I'll slice off your lips.'

Mathews fiddled with the handle of the room door, but gave up after a few seconds. Turned to walk away.

Prabu knew he had just one more chance. One chance only. His elbow was centimetres from an empty bottle of arrack on a table by the window. But he couldn't focus on it. As much as he tried, the bottle appeared to move away. He looked out through the glass door again and saw Mathews shielding his pipe from the rain.

It was a matter of seconds before he would be gone. Prabu dived at the table, tackling its legs so that the bottle slid off it and smashed against the floor next to his head. Shards of glass bounced against his cheeks.

Coach Silva dropped to his knees and stuck his forearm against Prabu's neck. 'Stay still, little bastard.'

Mathews walked back towards the room. He fiddled with the handle on the glass door and something clicked. Light broke into the room as the curtains blew in with the wind. Mathews looked towards Prabu, removed his glasses, rubbed his eyes and then looked again.

'Who did this?' He tried to pull the tennis ball out of Prabu's mouth. Prabu made some muffled noises. Pointed with his eyes towards Coach Silva, who rose to his feet out of Mathews' shadow.

Spitting out the tennis ball at last, Prabu, in the same breath, said, 'Behind you, behind you, behind you, beh—'

Mathews turned, raising his arms in defence. 'Coach, what the hell?'

'Mr Mathews, I can explain,' Coach Silva said.

A bolt of lightning lit the room.

'You horrible deviant,' Mathews said. 'What have you

gone and done? What have you gone and done? You've ruined everything.'

Prabu gasped for air and spat out yellow fibres from the tennis ball. Spat out vomit.

'Not what you think it is,' Coach Silva said. 'Didn't touch the boy. Swear on my wife.'

'Oh come off it,' Mathews said. 'It's bloody obvious.'

'No, no, no. Just caned him. Punished him.'

Mathews shuffled towards Prabu. Stroked his hair. 'God knows what this cantankerous old git did to you. We had such good plans.' He shook his head. 'Sorry, but I have no choice.' He yanked at Prabu's hair and rammed the tennis ball back into his mouth.

Prabu gagged on the ball, trying to scream; trying to breathe; trying to understand.

Mathews held Coach Silva by the chin. 'Do you think I'm an imbecile? You've shaved his chest.'

'Did that for you,' Coach said. 'The boy's for you.'

'I said I wanted fresh meat, and your hands have been all over him.'

'No, no, no. Never touched him. Never touched him.'

'Why Prabu?' Mathews asked. 'Why did you choose Prabu?'

'He's an orphan. No parents to talk to.'

'Screw talking to parents,' Mathews said. 'The little angel can't talk to anyone.'

'He won't.' Coach Silva smiled. 'I can promise you, he won't.'

Mathews started undoing his shirt. 'Well then Prabu's perfect. Now give us some privacy, Coach.'

TWENTY-FIVE

Prabu had drunk alcohol before. Been destroyed by a couple of glasses of the hard stuff. But now he had been forced to drink like a man.

It hurt behind his eyes, under his tongue, inside his ears. He felt like he had things crawling under his skin.

Every time he threw up into the squat toilet, he glugged water from the hand shower. With time, he felt better, but he also remembered more and more. More about Coach Silva. More about Mathews.

He knew what he had to do.

After a shower and a change of clothes, he lay on the bed, a pillow under each armpit, his head up like a cobra's. His eyes open, it felt like he was looking through cheap, cloudy marbles.

He faced the door, watching Indika as he entered. Unsteady on his legs, smelling of cigarette smoke. Returning from a day of boozing on the beach with friends. The way it should be.

Mosquitoes buzzed around Prabu's bare legs but he didn't even try to fan them away.

'Machan, how?' Indika asked. Slurred.

Prabu tilted his head towards him, shutting his eyes, which squeezed a tear out to run down his face.

Sitting down on the bed, Indika put a hand on Prabu's back.

Flinching, Prabu jerked his head back and grabbed Indika's wrist. 'Sorry, brother. I'm ...'

'No news about yourself?'

Prabu stood up. 'Not selected.'

Indika shook his head. 'Don't believe it.'

Had it been anyone else, Prabu may have been annoyed by the condescending bad-luck-machan pat on the back, but he knew Indika meant well. 'From where I was few months ago, I can make a happy with what I have.'

'Someone will get injured,' Indika said. 'Someone will lose form.'

'Maybe.'

Indika bowed his head, closed his eyes, then looked up and held Prabu's hand. 'Give it time, machan. Times are changing. Play out of your skin and they'll pick you eventually.'

'They won't.'

Indika lay down on the bed, saying nothing. Prabu feared he may have driven him away. He was about to walk out of the room, but then Indika, eyes still closed, patted the bed on a spot right next to him. Prabu thought about it for a second and then eased on to a corner of the mattress, making sure they didn't touch each other.

He said, 'Maybe it's better if I go home.'

Indika switched off the light. 'We're going home tomorrow.'

'I mean, my home, home. Where I'm same as others.'

Rolling on to his back, Indika crossed his arms over his chest. 'The north?'

Prabu could see Indika's lips and chin, but shadows obscured the rest of his face, making him look like Batman.

'Anywhere.'

Indika took a deep breath and put one hand on Prabu's shoulder. 'I'll never let them take you back.' He sat up, flicked on the light. 'I'm not an idiot, Prabu. I know you're a much better player than me.'

Prabu grunted.

'Look, it's obvious. I hate cricket anyway. I'm just living out my father's dreams.'

'But you make the team,' Prabu said.

'It's a con. No way I can be in and not you. Sometimes I know I have to do well or Thathi will mope around the house. But I wish I could just fail. Just be done with cricket. Be sent to England. Maybe date Isabella there, you know.'

'You still make a turn on for her?'

Indika grinned. 'Will always make a turn on for her.' He switched the light off, slipping down the plastic-covered mattress. Within seconds his snoring sounded like the engine of an overloaded trishaw.

Prabu had never felt closer to him. Never felt this close to anyone since his mother left.

He waited till he could hear the gentle sounds of the low-tide waves above Indika's snoring. In the dim light of the half-moon that snaked through the torn curtains, he packed his bag and walked to the door.

Lying on his stomach, Indika had his face side-on to the pillow, pushing his open mouth into the shape of a fish's.

Prabu couldn't bear to leave, but he knew he had no choice, given what he was about to do. It would threaten the goal of why he was at school in Colombo, but he could find another way to succeed.

He tiptoed back to the bed. Pulling the scorebook Thathi had given him out of his bag, he tore out the page that tallied his highest ever partnership with Indika. On the back he wrote 'Always my brother'.

He sat on the floor, watching Indika sleep for more than twenty minutes. At least Indika would not have the chance to abandon him. At least Prabu would have some memories he didn't spend his whole life trying to forget.

He sneaked out of the room, locked the door from the outside. Slipped the key under it.

He turned the handle of the door to the room at the end of the corridor. 'I'm ready.' He limped to the middle of the room, took off his shirt, slapped his own face. 'I told to you I come back.'

'I'll make it worth your while,' Mathews said.

Prabu marched towards him and grabbed him by the neck. Kicked his legs out from under him. Dropped him to the red polished floor.

'What the hell are you—'

'Shut up.' Prabu wrapped his t-shirt around his fist. 'Shut up or I kill you.'

'Prabu, please, I can't control myself. I become someone else, and I don't like that—'

Bang. A punch so hard into Mathews' jaw that it dislodged a tooth.

'I'm a good man,' Mathews said. Crying. 'I need help.'

Bang. Bang. Bang.

Mathews howling. Trying to get his arms up to defend his face.

Bang. Bang. Bang.

'Coach Silva is not tell you I am tortured, right?' Prabu said, Mathews' blood on his cheeks.

'I am taken in by army.' Prabu, a smile on his face, started stretching his hamstrings, his sides, his lats. 'First time they get me, they torture me. Try to find out what I know.'

Bang. Bang. Bang.

'You know what they do? They make me put my dick inside of a drawer and they kick it shut if I tell to them a lie.'

'Please, please,' Mathews said, his hands by his face in prayer.

Prabu pulled Mathews up off the floor. 'But I got a lucky. Before they have a time to slam the drawer, Colonel Thisara is come in. Save me, like I thought you would save me.'

'Please, I meant to—'

'Do you think anyone will save you?' Prabu checked that the door was locked. Wedged a chair up against the handle to make sure.

'I'll give you money.'

Pulling out each drawer in the cupboard, Prabu gave

Mathews the thumbs up. 'This one is good height, no?'

'All my money.'

'Take off your trouser and panties.'

Hands on Prabu's shoulder. 'Anything, please, please.'

'Put your dick in that drawer.'

'No, I won't,' Mathews said.

'Then I kill you.'

'Okay, okay.' Mathews pulled down the front of his trousers and his pants. Placed the end of his penis in the drawer.

'All of it,' Prabu said. 'Balls too.'

'Okay, okay, but not too hard, right? I stopped when you asked me to.'

'What?' Prabu stretched his legs. 'I want you to never start. You know how much of the alcohol Coach Silva is pour down my throat.'

'I'm an old man.'

The scream must have woken up the whole hotel. By the time Prabu had cleared the wall on to the road, he could still hear it.

The bus to Colombo tilted to its right, as men and women jostled for space that wasn't there. Prabu hung out the door with his face in the conductor's armpit. Rain splattered against him, through the beams of the odd street light that worked.

The first stop was a mere fifty metres from where Prabu had got on. A Buddhist monk wanted to get off, so Prabu was pushed off the bus to make way. New passengers shoved their way on. The bus started moving before Prabu could get a foothold, so he chased after it until a stray dog started nipping at his ankles.

Prabu tripped over a pothole, ending up on his back, the dog's face inches from his.

He took a chance and tickled the dog under the chin. A new friendship was established.

He walked back to the bus stop, on the roof of which was a poster advertising the cricket match that his team had just won.

He flicked a ten-rupee coin at a juggling one-armed beggar, turned on his heel and ran back towards the guesthouse, even though it was far enough away to require a trishaw ride.

Jogging down to the beach, he could see his teammates in the distance, crouched in a circle around a campfire. Prabu wasn't ready to join them. Instead, he turned back to the guesthouse and watched Coach Silva handing some money to a policeman as an ambulance drove off behind them.

TWENTY-SIX

I see you as you march, legs straight, arms swinging high. You have new purpose.

The Supreme Leader grins when you enter his tent. 'Sit.'

Normally you would ask where. Now you choose your spot. 'I'm ready.'

'Have you seen one of these before?' The Supreme Leader hands you an iPad.

You wonder if it is a detonator. A high-tech piece of military equipment. Radar, night vision. Hell maybe it's a friggin' gun. 'No, sir.'

'Mr Majestyk will show you how to use it.' The Supreme Leader swipes a hand across the screen and icons pop up. This is serious James Bond shit, you think.

A lion roars, and music starts blaring. 'What's this?'

'Movies. We've loaded *Death Wish*, parts 1 and 2. We've loaded the *Dirty Dozen, Guns of Navarone* and *Rambo*. You heard of *Rambo*?'

'Seen a poster.'

'Now you see the films,' the Supreme Leader says. 'Classics. A one-man destruction machine.'

'To inspire me?'

Giggling, high-pitched, the Supreme Leader kisses you on the cheeks. 'No, to inspire, you watch *Rocky*. Watch the training montages. It'll make you stronger, faster, train harder, become a bloody rock.'

Sweet friggin' Jesus, you love *Rocky*. The Supreme Leader was in the know. Right. The training scenes make you sprint faster. They make you run with a friggin' tree on your shoulders, make you think about swimming, but you're still scared of the water.

You shoulder-press a bullock cart with four men in it, and while they smile, you roar. The roar of a wounded tiger. The roar of a man not a boy. The warning to Sinhalese murderers; you're coming for them.

So you do weights. But you're not getting bigger because you're on the run and you're short on food. You can't kill animals as it makes you sad. But you know you can kill a bunch of Sinhalese kids.

And you have to ditch the weights because your backpack tears, and Mr Majestyk, the last man with you, says it's holding you guys up.

There's a rumour that the Supreme Leader has been caught. The word on the battlefield is that he surrendered, but you know that's a lie. He's too strong for that. Too brave.

Mr Majestyk is limping. Struggling physically, but even more mentally.

'It's over,' he says. 'We're dead.'

You want to slap him for giving up. For being weak. But you try to give him hope. 'I'll get you out of here.'

'I think we should surrender. Then they'll have more time to trust you. You can get—'

'No surrender,' you say. 'Not yet.'

But you wake up in a tree and you see Mr Majestyk, arms in the air, white flag spread between his hands. Limping into No Moustache Land. *Bloody coward,* you think.

A small bang, a whistle, a bullet through his head. A bullet in his chest. He drops to his knees, hands on his face. A bullet through his friggin' hand and eye. Bang. His face in the mud. His white flag floating down on to his body.

Never friggin' surrender, you tell yourself. *Just get faster. Just get better. What doesn't kill you can only make you stronger.*

And now you're alone again, until you find Toyota. The white stray dog who shares your food. The dog the same colour as the white Toyota van in which you were first brought in when you became a man. An urban Panther.

You're doing your push-ups. You're doing your pull-ups from the branches of trees. You're doing shuttle runs and leaps.

You're an athletic super machine.

They will never catch you.

You're friggin' John Rambosingham.

You can smell the stale arrack on the soldier's breath. A bead of his sweat falls on your outstretched arm. Your hands hold together the wide leaves in front of you. Without their cover, you're dead.

'I think no one is here,' the soldier says. 'Just the animals.' He turns to walk away, but hops to the side when Toyota runs past him and sniffs right next to you; his head burrows under the leaves. His teeth are inches from you. You tickle Toyota's neck. He licks your wrist and bends down to eat your vomit. Backing away, he shakes the beach's sand off his back.

'Putha,' a commander says, 'the dog's tail is wagging. Check what he's seen.' The soldier turns to walk towards you again. You think you may have made eye contact with the soldier, but maybe his eyesight is weak. You must stay still.

Toyota growls at the soldier as he gets closer to you. The soldier jumps back and pulls out his gun; he's threatening your dog. But Toyota advances on him, to say sorry, you think. Not to attack. Toyota's a lovable idiot. Loves everyone, even if they try to kill him.

His nose points down near the ground, and his tail swings from side to side.

BANG. Howl. Toyota lies limp in his own blood. Shit.

You jump on to your bare feet but your gun is on the other side of the bush.

A gunshot. You don't know where from.

'Don't shoot, you idiot,' the commander says.

Chariots of Fire theme music in your head. Sprint, you little bugger. Life or death. You turn left on the beach and run, chest puffed out, arms pumping, your legs like jelly, because it's real. Not just training.

You run straight into an outstretched arm at neck height. Your legs slide forward in the sand and you land on your back. You look up, but can't make out the face of the man standing above you. But before he can lift his gun, you ram your head into his nuts.

You can make out the silhouette of another man in front of you. So your only choice is the sea, and water freaks you out. What would Amma say?

You dive, head first, over a churning wave. Your chest lands on coral. It stings like shit. You try to stand. More coral. You need to stay afloat and not make contact with the ground. A small wave smacks you down. Under. You can't see past your eyelashes. The water tucks you up and rolls you over.

You stand again on rocks. Another wave takes out your legs. It's like a friggin' washing machine.

You have to swim past this. No choice. Another running dive and you swim underwater. Less waves this way. You hold your breath for what seems like a minute and use a wide, shallow breaststroke. Thank god they made you practise swimming, even if it was on land.

Every few seconds you hear the whoosh of new waves passing over the surface and feel a rush of water on your back. It's strong but you're stronger. You lift your head up. Facing out to sea. A good seventy-five metres out. Safe from the soldiers, but how the hell will you survive? Get back to shore?

You know you're bleeding. You remember that blood attracts sharks. Are there sharks here? You have nowhere to go.

Your choices are limited. Drown at sea or be taken in by Sinhalese murderers. You feel weak. Little breath left in you. Seawater in the hollow between your nose and mouth. Your legs are abandoning you. They seem ready to give up and move on to another life.

You watch a wave coming towards you and close your eyes. You go underwater and try to ride this wave. It takes you ashore but you scrape your chest on more dead coral.

No pain, no gain.

You get on your feet and run through the water on to the beach. You can hear muffled voices and the dull sound of feet pounding sand.

Lift the knees high. Head upright. Pump the arms. Run like hell. Fast. Fast. Fast.

In your head you're an Olympic sprinter, all dressed up and vying for medals. But the noises get closer, then farther away.

Then the gunfire and the soldiers drop dead to the ground below a flare that lights up the beach.

And you are called over to a bush. In Tamil.

The man pushes your head down on to his lap. 'Keep quiet.'

A row of men, all with machine guns. Firing at the soldiers.

'You're Panthers?'

The man lifts your head back up, nods. 'Go to the back.'

You start moving. Then you see his face. You want to hug him, kiss his feet, cry on his shoulder. But he lifts a finger to his mouth.

'Shush, don't say anything.' The man stands, fires off a round of bullets and as he passes you, he says, 'I love you, son.'

TWENTY-SEVEN

Passing through the construction work for the country's first motorway, Thathi drove while Ammi sat in the back, massaging Indika, who sat in front of her.

'This is it, son,' Thathi said. 'Your last chance to break all the under-seventeen records.'

'I don't know about that,' Indika said. 'All set by that Jamaican exchange student.'

'Yes, but we have a secret weapon.'

Ammi squeezed Indika's deltoids. 'Tell him, tell him.'

'We have incredible inefficiency on our side.' Thathi tapped Indika on the leg. 'The reason this track cannot be considered for international events is because they cocked it up. It's too damn short.'

Prabu laughed. 'Cannot be, no Uncle?'

'Did you get an email about this?' Indika asked. 'We told you, those emails aren't true.'

'Look, it's true, okay. This was earmarked for the Commonwealth Games if we won the bid, but they rushed it.'

'I still have to win the race, though,' Indika said.

'Judging by the field you're up against, that's a formality.' Thathi adjusted his mirror to look at Prabu. 'What events have you been entered for?'

'Uncle, I am not so much aware. My house captain said that she will tell to me when I am arrive.'

'What events do you want to do?' Ammi asked.

'Anything. As long as I am not have to do one hundred, two hundred or long jump.' He pointed to Indika. 'Then I am have no chance against him.'

Indika said, 'Prabu's good at long distances, so I reckon they'll put him down for the eight hundred and one thousand five. We're in the same house, so maybe we can cleansweep all the track events.'

'Well, putha,' Thathi said, 'don't bother coming home unless you win all your events. Bloody embarrassing if you lose to these punks.'

'Have you been taking bets with other parents again?' Indika asked.

'No comment.'

Two soldiers saluted Thathi, then opened the gate to the stadium, which certainly looked the part, with an Olympic flame on a bank overlooking the track. Stray dogs played in the long jump sandpit, and a cow grazed near the pole vault mat, but on the whole, the army had maintained the ground well. The government used thousands of soldiers, heroes a year or so ago, to instil their discipline into ramshackle public entities.

When Indika got out of the jeep, his house captain ran to him and draped a flag over his shoulders. She turned to Prabu and informed him that he would be running the eight hundred and fifteen hundred as expected, but also the hundred and two hundred.

'Why are you making him do the sprints?' Indika asked, in a high-pitched voice. He corrected this, overcompensating with a Mr T tone. 'He's a long-distance runner.'

The house captain looked flustered. 'Please, Indi, I'm confused enough. Everyone else is down for their maximum four events. His name's in already.'

Prabu flicked through the programme for the day and laughed. 'I have to do one five and eight hundred before two hundred and one hundred. Sometimes I could be dead by then.'

The eight hundred metres race was first, and in a reasonably strong field of mostly footballers, Prabu lay second from last with a lap to go. Running barefoot, he came around the last bend, passed the grazing cow, and moved to third. Regardless of house allegiances, everyone united in their cheering of Prabu. The buzz around the stadium drowned out Mr Carter's comic commentary on the loud speaker.

Prabu slowed to look around. Achala skipped to the side of the track to cheer him on, and Indika appeared too nervous to say anything.

Prabu held his breath, closed his eyes and concentrated on lengthening his stride. Opening his eyes, he saw the leader's heels kick up two metres in front of him. Moving one lane out, he put his head down, sprinting, gasping in air that didn't seem to be there. He pumped his chest out as he crossed the line, a hundredth of a second in front of the athletics captain.

The Papare band started playing a jumble of horns and drums. Indika got to Prabu first, lifting him off the ground with a bear hug that showed everyone that he was the stronger of the two. Or thought he was.

In contrast, the long jump was a low-key affair. In fact, Indika's support was limited to his parents, Prabu, the sandpit dogs and an eleven-year-old who stalked Indika pretty much wherever he went.

Indika's first jump fell well short of the record set by the Jamaican exchange student, but a good foot ahead of Bong Hwa who finished in second place. Indika fouled his next two jumps, on Thathi's insistence that he had to break the record. He won, of course, but Thathi wasn't impressed.

When Mr Carter announced the fifteen hundred, everyone gathered near the finish line. Before the firing of the starter's pistol, the crowd screamed out Prabu's name. He peeked out of the corner of his eye at the boy on his left, knowing that he had won this event at the inter-international sports meet.

The gun fired, the crowd went wild.

Prabu felt something fuzzy in his head. It made him happy. It made him determined. It made him strong.

He kicked his legs up, his heels almost touching his backside as he drove to stretch his stride. He stormed straight to the front of the pack, closed his eyes on the first straight and chanted 'Indi, Indi, Indi' to himself. He knew victory in this race would mean so much to his great friend.

The more impact Prabu made at school, the less chance there was of them kicking him out even if he failed his exams. He hoped. He knew he had to win and win big.

He clenched his fists and sucked in huge breaths. As he came to the bend, he opened his eyes, rotated his head and saw the rest of the field fifty or so metres behind. Chasing him.

Every time he had been chased before he had been caught or saved by someone else.

Not this time. This was his.

He couldn't tire. He pictured his mother and sister at the finishing line, getting ready to leave without him again.

Focused, he drove into a gear he didn't know he had. The crowd roared out his name, which made him go even faster.

Teachers and timekeepers lined up at the finishing line. His vision opaque, he saw hands waving and people jumping. He crossed the line and couldn't stop himself from almost knocking over Principal Uncle.

Principal Uncle bent down to shake his hand. 'Son, that was the greatest exhibition of running I have ever seen in my twenty-two years at this school.'

Prabu failed to control his whimper.

Thathi looked at Principal Uncle and said, 'Wait till you see Indika in the one hundred metres.'

Indika stood on Prabu's feet, grabbed his hands and pulled him up.

The blue ribbon event. The hundred metres. The eight

runners, two from each house, lined up in either orange, green, red or blue shirts. Indika and Prabu were in lanes two and six respectively.

Thathi slapped Indika's back, making him flinch. 'Jayanettis don't lose. Humiliate the others. You're a winner.'

'And a warrior,' Indika said.

'Eat them up,' Thathi said.

'With chilli paste.'

'I love you, putha.' Thathi turned to Prabu. 'Try your best.'

Crouching, looking down at his lane, Prabu imagined the music from *Chariots of Fire*, which he had watched again with Indika the night before. He remembered how Indika trained for his starts. Don't get fully upright too fast, pump the hands, lift the knees high. Get rhythm.

Prabu felt strange in a crouched start position. The shoes Indika had given him for this race seemed too tight, so he kicked them off and stood upright.

Take your marks ...

Prabu turned slightly to see Indika speaking to himself in his crouched stance.

Set ...

Indika put his head down ...

Fire ...

Indika flew out of the blocks and stretched away from the others.

Prabu could see his calf muscles bouncing him off the track.

The crowd howled as if possessed.

Prabu, Prabu, Prabu, Prabu …

He felt himself getting closer to Indika.

Prabu, Prabu, Prabu, Prabu …

On his left he could see a flash of straight hair and fair skin. He could see arms pumping, robotic. He could hear Indika's breaths, powerful like a storm.

Prabu closed his eyes, screamed a little, and threw his chest forward past the line. Ran straight to Indika, said, 'Well done, champ.'

'Bugger off, you monkey,' Indika said. 'Don't take the bloody piss.'

The crowd mobbed Prabu, which was when he realized he had won.

Prabu had broken another school record.

Indika lay on the ground clutching at his leg.

Thathi bent over him. 'Knee playing up again?'

'Yes, Thathi, yes, and it hurts like hell.'

'So unlucky,' Thathi said.

Prabu felt guilty. He knew he had won only because Indika got injured. He saw how much it upset Ammi and Thathi.

Prior to the two hundred metres, Prabu followed Indika, who had his right knee heavily strapped as he limped towards Mr Carter.

'Could you please announce for the crowd to be quiet at starter's orders?' Indika said. 'I couldn't hear the pistol for the hundred.'

'You got a hell of a start though, champ. You lost it in the last fifty.'

'My knee, sir, sorry.'

'Don't apologize to me. As long as someone broke the record.'

Indika blocked Prabu's view of Mr Carter's face. 'Will the record stand, sir? Even though it was heavily wind-assisted?' Indika asked.

'What do you think this is, the Olympics? Of course it stands.'

'Isn't the track too short?'

'Focus on the two hundred, okay, or I may just lose a bit of respect for you. Your dad's sent me about fifteen text messages saying the same thing. And, look, if I'm honest, it's ugly.'

Indika seemed to be in agony at the starting line for the two hundred metres. He howled out in pain with every step that he took. Adding extra strapping around his knee, he sprayed the bandages with Deep Heat.

Ready …

Set …

Indika threw his hand up. 'Wait, sir.' He stood upright and kicked his right leg out in front of him. 'I don't know if I can run. It's agony.'

'Okay, mate, no worries,' Mr Carter said. 'Move aside and I'll start the others.'

'Wait, wait, sir. Let me just try. I'll do my best.'

Prabu stood, open-mouthed, as the wind whistled through the gaps in his teeth. Indika's strength and courage inspired him.

He jogged over to Indika and held him up at the waist.
'Keep weight off knee, brother.'

'I'll try my best, machan. This means so much to Ammi
and Thathi. Break their hearts if I lost the hundred and
the two hundred on the same day.'

'Sorry that I won the hundred.'

'Guys, are you ready?' Mr Carter asked.

Indika said, 'Just one minute please, sir.' He put
his mouth to Prabu's ear, tickling him with his breath.
'Machan, I know you didn't mean to. Obviously, staying
at our house, eating our food and coming in our jeep, you
wouldn't have planned to beat me. I guess the wind must
have pushed you over against your will.'

Prabu moved his gaze away from Indika. He couldn't
look at Indika after he had betrayed him this way.

Starting in lane three, he could see Indika in front of
him in lane seven.

Mr Carter fired the pistol. Prabu flew past the runners
in lanes four and five. Round the bend he gobbled up the
runners in lanes six and eight. He felt like Pac-Man.

Achala said that God would be on Prabu's side but she
was wrong for once. It was obvious whose side he was
on when Indika's limp vanished. When Indika regained
full motion of his legs.

Prabu slowed down because he didn't want to risk the
wind carrying him over again.

He saw Indika cross the line and he leapt for joy mid-
race.

The crowd remained silent, but Indika burst through

his parents' hugs, turned to high-five Prabu as he crossed the line in third place

If possible, he sprinted even faster on his victory lap. Prabu's smile resembled the curve of the two hundred metre track itself, as he witnessed the miracle of Indika's knee recovery again. Even though the bandages had come off, Indika showed no pain. Prabu could not believe his friend's strength.

Mr Carter announced that Indika had broken the school record.

Eventually Prabu caught up with Indika and hugged him.

'Bad luck, machan,' Indika said. 'No wind this time?'

TWENTY-EIGHT

For once, Prabu didn't miss his best friend. Holding Achala's hand, he had to fight to keep from skipping down the cobblestone streets within the walls of Galle Fort.

Achala stopped and spun around on her heel, tapping an English expatriate on the shoulder to ask him if he would complete a survey for their fieldwork.

She passed her camera to Prabu, who photographed the buildings painted in burnt orange.

The survey completed, Achala grabbed Prabu's hand, dragging him up to the thick fort walls. The sea beat against the rocks, splashing salt across Prabu's newly divided eyebrows.

Achala brushed the back of her hand across his face. Pinched his cheeks.

No, he certainly didn't miss Indika.

Later, they sat on a sofa at the back of an art gallery that served mango cheesecake.

Prabu had never felt like this before in his life. The

perfect girl stroking the hairs on his arms. The signs looked good. At least the signs that Indika had told Prabu to look out for.

Achala played with her hair a lot; she opened and closed her eyelids at the speed of a butterfly's flapping wings; she tilted her head down to look up at him. 'Would you like it if we became, you know …?' she asked.

Prabu struggled to speak. This seemed to be happening even faster than he had plotted in his optimistic diary. He had expected what had happened so far; sitting next to her on the coach journey; tabulating data with her. But this? So soon? He squeezed her hands tighter but couldn't get the words out.

Achala spoke. 'Take things slow, but you know, commit to each other?'

Prabu forced out a smile, maybe the hardest one he had ever given. 'I love …'

'You love what?'

He knew he couldn't say it. Too early. Too keen. All the warnings the six single boys of the Scorpion Five had given him. 'I love the idea.'

'You get me, Prabu, you get me like only Daddy does. You're like my best girlfriend.'

'I am not a girl, no.' Prabu said.

'You'd be a hot girl.'

'Please to stop calling me a girl.'

She closed her eyes and edged forward. 'Make me.'

Prabu bobbed his head towards her. Stuck out his lips, but just before contact could have been made, Achala pulled away.

She said, 'God spoke to me this morning. He dropped me a speck of silver on my lips and told me that tonight someone would kiss me, and through that kiss, a relationship would be born that would lead to another child of Jesus.'

Prabu held his breath. Went in for a kiss again.

Achala put a finger to his lips. 'He said it would be under the light of the moon. Tonight.'

Prabu let the breath out of his mouth fast enough to blow Achala's fringe to one side.

Prabu sought out Indika, who he found with the other members of the Scorpion Five, sitting on the walls of Galle Fort, looking out over the sea. Each had his own can of beer as they passed around two cigarettes between them.

'You're losing your hold, Indika,' Founding Scorpion Gajen said. 'Here comes Prabu, the fan's favourite now.'

'Even looks like he'll score Achala,' said rice-bellied Scorpion Gayan. 'You never managed that, no?'

Muslim Scorpion Kuzi played with his candyfloss beard. 'Scored more runs than you last season. Lots more.'

Vain Scorpion Rajiv said, 'More newspaper articles about him and not just because he's Tamil.' He dabbed gel in his spiky hair. 'Been on the BBC, which you never have.'

Mixed-race Scorpion Shoban flapped out his leather jacket. 'Beat you in the hundred metres. All these things were unthinkable. He's younger than you, he's had no coaching, he's poor, but he's taking over your life.'

Prabu said, 'You are a silly. Indika is the Papadum King.'

Gajen smiled. 'Not for long.'

'Hell,' Rajiv said, 'even his parents seem to like you more.'

All the Scorpions laughed. They shared chest bumps that Prabu tried to watch and copy but it seemed like they didn't quite know what they were doing themselves.

Indika framed his chin with his right hand, said, 'But the Papadum King needs to be beautiful, like me.'

Gayan said, 'Vomit. If you're so sexy, how come you could never get Achala?'

'I could have had her any time,' Indika said, 'just didn't want her.'

Prabu knew this may have been true, but it hurt him to think about it. Achala claimed she hated Indika, but then again, who didn't love the Papadum King?

'The Papadum Dance of December 2009,' Rajiv said, 'when you gave her red roses, you didn't want her then?'

'Gifting her a couple of discounted flowers means nothing. Got two for the price of—'

'You gave her three hundred.'

'Got three hundred for the price of two.'

The Scorpions laughed.

Gayan said, 'The Christian beauty blew you off.'

'Look, guys,' Indika pulled out the gang handshake. 'She was in a different place then. Only man in her life was'—he signalled inverted commas—'Daddy.'

Gajen said, 'Well Prabu must be doing a good Daddy impression.'

'If I tried it on with her now, she'd be putty in my hands.' Indika unleashed some finger snapping and unanswered high fives before turning to Prabu. 'Just joking, machan. Now she has eyes only for you. But I could have had her before. If. I. Wanted.'

'It's all just noise to me,' Gajen said, 'unless you prove it.'

'How can he prove?' Prabu grabbed a cigarette from Shoban. 'Just believe him, okay?'

'Prabu's in love. I'm not going to mess with that.'

'Pussy,' Gajen said.

'Pussy, pussy, pussy, pussy, pussy,' said the others.

'Okay, okay,' Indika said. 'Look, I'm not interested in her any more.'

'Because you can't get her,' Gayan said. 'Just like you couldn't beat Prabu in the hundred metres.'

'I didn't hear the starter's pistol.'

'What's your excuse now?'

'Pussy. Pussy. Pussy. Pussy.'

'You're the pussies. Listen, you gay boys, I don't screw with my friends' girls.'

'Yes, he would never do that,' Prabu said.

Indika stood up, downed the rest of his beer and jumped off the fort wall on to the cobblestone street. 'Bloody childish fellows you are,' he said, as he slipped into his self-branded leather jacket in thirty-six-degree heat.

In the Maritime Museum, Prabu broke away from Achala and grabbed Indika by the arm. 'Brother, I have some news. But I am not so much sure I can tell you.'

Indika had his phone in his hand, texting someone. 'Okay then, no worries.'

'God has made himself available in a vision for Achala and told her that tonight she will make her first kiss.'

Indika put his phone in his pocket. 'Jesus.'

'No. God, not Jesus.' Prabu smiled, ducking his head towards Indika's ear. 'I am spending tonight, when we go to that fancy ass hotel, with Achala. I will take her to the swimming pool and then maybe I shall make a kiss. Under the moon.'

'This is all because God told her?'

'Correct.'

Indika sat down, hands on his lap. 'You believe it?'

'She have a very good communication with God and his son. I believe it.'

'So it's your destiny?'

Keeping his mouth closed, Prabu giggled in the high-pitched manner he found hard to control. 'Must be, brother. I am very excite. Never I have thought one day I can kiss a girl with her approval.'

Eating dinner at the Lighthouse Hotel, on a cliff against which waves crashed and spat up water like inverted rain, Prabu did everything he could to make Achala like him more. He served her food, topped up her drinks even when she said she was done; wiped seawater off her face when it splashed her.

He knew he had to be careful not to get too happy. Whenever things seemed to be going well in his life, something would go wrong. But here, he felt safe. He had Indika, and soon he would have Achala.

When Mr Carter went to the bathroom, leaving the students unattended, Indika approached him at the station at which a sweaty chef cooked egg hoppers. 'Machan, you want her by the pool, no?'

Prabu nodded so much his head looked like it would fall off.

'Leave it to me.'

TWENTY-NINE

Walking down the stairs to the first of the two swimming pools, Prabu whistled a Kool and the Gang song until he was frightened within an inch of sharting by Gayan jumping out from behind a coconut tree.

'Hey, machan,' he said. 'Maybe you don't want to go down there.'

Achala and Indika faced each other by the second pool. They swayed to music under a palm tree that shone the light of the moon off the fingers of its leaves.

Prabu crept towards them, away from the Scorpions who skulled arrack on the steps of the spa.

He hid behind a coconut tree, like an estranged lover in a Hindi film.

Achala kept turning back to the rock stairs leading down from the other pool. Prabu assumed she was looking for him, which made him feel like he had never felt before.

Indika grabbed her shoulder and turned her around to face him. 'You know, during the tsunami, that pool and the spa by it went completely under.'

'Did anyone die?'

'I'm not sure to be honest. Gish told me no one did, but he also told me a crocodile saved an old man from drowning during the tsunami, so I'm sceptical.'

Achala looked up at the stars. 'What did you want to tell me?'

Indika wrapped his hands around her little fingers. 'Prabu's had a tough life. You seem to have cheered him up.'

Achala pulled her hands free, tied her hair up in a bun, her face looking like a second moon. 'I think you can take some credit for that too.'

'Please promise you won't hurt him.'

'Of course not.

Prabu followed Indika's gaze towards where the Scorpions crouched like crabs.

'The thing is,' Indika said, 'I used to like you so much and I thought you were the one. I really did.'

'But I—'

'Please just let me finish. I realized it wasn't to be. Out of my league.'

Achala untied her hair and flicked it across her face like she had done when she sat with Prabu for lunch. 'Don't be silly.'

Bowing his head, Indika chuckled. 'I'm shy to ask, but—'

'I wasn't immune to your charm,' Achala said. 'But you had a bad reputation. You would have had no respect for me.'

'As if.' Indika bunched up the sleeves of his leather jacket. 'I knew you deserved better.'

'Than the hunk of Colombo? Don't be silly.'

Indika directed a thumbs up towards the Scorpions. He ran a hand over Achala's dyed brown hair. 'I could have loved you, but I guess it wasn't destined by God, and I'm so happy you've found Prabu.'

Achala grinned. 'That's so sweet and honourable of you.'

'Prabu will be here shortly, so I'll leave you to it.' He kissed her on both cheeks. 'Besides, maybe my luck is about to change too. Sadly not with you, it seems.'

'With who? One of those loose white women?'

'I don't know.' Indika laughed. 'This may sound crazy, but I could swear I had a visitation from our lord last night. Maybe it was all just a dream, but ...'

'What did he say?'

'It's so odd. I couldn't make it all out, but something about the person I would spend the rest of my life with.'

'Yes, and?' Achala asked.

Indika looked up towards the stars. 'How we would kiss under the moon ...'

Prabu saw Achala's smile vanish. Replaced by a look he couldn't describe. He started headbutting the tree, knowing that once again he had been deceived. Betrayed.

'You're bloody kidding me,' Achala said.

Indika lifted his hands up as if he had a gun pointed at him. 'What?'

'The lord, under whose feet I worship, visited me and told me the very same thing.'

Indika's gaze fixed on her. 'Oh my bloody go ... nads.'

Achala, hands on Indika's shoulders, asked, 'You know what this means?'

Indika frowned, narrowed his eyes and shook his head. 'That we both have to kiss Prabu?'

'No, silly,' Achala laughed. 'It means you and I are destined to kiss.' She moved to embrace Indika, but he raised his hands and pressed them against her shoulders.

'If this is destined ...' He rocked forward. Locked his lips on hers.

A real snog.

With tongue.

Prabu stopped breathing. Pounded his fists into the palm tree, accidentally knocking the tail off a gecko in the process. Tasted shit between his teeth. The smell of flesh. War.

He pulled at his own hair. Bolted towards Indika. Spat on his shoes.

He kicked off his flip-flops. Leapt over the boundary wall on to the beach. Looking one way and then the other, he charged across the sand, diving into shallow water.

His life was over. There was nothing worth living for. Again, the two people he loved most had betrayed him; had abandoned him; had broken his heart.

After snorting some salt water, Prabu crawled his way back on to the sand. He wanted to go back to the camp. He could end up there for the rest of his life, but at least Colonel Thisara wanted him. At least he had worth there.

He saw Indika jogging on the beach towards him.

That's all I mean to the Papadum King. Just a jog.

'I let you win, you stupid bastard,' Prabu shouted.

He had no idea if Indika heard or not.

THIRTY

Prabu looked over the edge of the cliff by the swimming pool at the Mount Lavinia Hotel. On the beach below, Kandyan dancers strutted their stuff to the rhythmic booms of colourful drums. A blonde bride, dressed in a sari, followed them on an elephant.

Under the red-tinged sky, the sun setting into the sea, the dancers cart-wheeled across the sand.

'This is where they filmed the hospital scene in *The Bridge on the River Kwai*,' Thathi said.

Indika and Prabu failed to respond.

'I wonder if we should leave the boys alone,' Ammi said.

'Please do,' Indika said.

Prabu shook his head. Stood to speak to Thathi. 'I'm sorry. I try not to offer you disrespect, but I not so much sure I can speak with your son.'

'You've punished him enough,' Thathi said. 'He's been inconsolable for the last couple of weeks and his cricket is really suffering because of it. I don't need to know what happened, but you must realize what you're doing to his dream of playing for Sri Lanka.'

'That's your dream, Tha.'

Thathi ran his hand through Indika's hair. 'If that helps take the pressure off, then think that way. But Prabu, I beg of you. I want to see my son happy again.'

'You look after me,' Prabu said. 'You make me feel fitted in. But I want to go home. The God does not mean for me to be here. I want to go home, Uncle.'

'I need to tell you what happened,' Indika said.

'I don't need to know,' Thathi said.

'Not you. I need to tell Prabu. I keep trying, but ...'

'Please,' Ammi said. 'Give him half an hour. Even if you don't think he deserves it, maybe you would agree that we do. Please.'

Prabu rolled his head in a figure of eight. That meant okay.

After Ammi and Thathi went through the glass doors back to the lobby, Prabu stood, watching the priest chanting at the Poruwa ceremony. The white lady in the sari had been joined on the podium by a sunburnt bald man dressed as a Kandyan king.

Indika closed his eyes. Lifted his hands in prayer. 'Please, machan.'

Prabu forced out a fake smile as he watched the bride drop betel leaves on the Poruwa.

'At least listen,' Indika said. 'You don't even need to say anything.'

Prabu turned a rattan chair away from Indika and the table. Facing the sunset, he said, 'Talk, then.'

'There's no escape from what I did. I've thought of a million excuses, but it'll just make things worse. You must know I don't even talk to Achala any more. She means—'

'Bull and shit,' Prabu said.

'Only interested because I couldn't have her. The last few months haven't been easy for me either. I'm not used to losing anything and—'

'You want me to cry for you?' Prabu kicked his chair away and stood up, aware of the dirty looks on the faces of the Europeans sipping gin-and-tonics by the pool. 'Sad bloody life for you, no? Too much of money? Too much of chances? Black bloody Tamil boy comes and beats you in a race and you cry?'

Indika stood, lifting his finger to his mouth. 'Please, Prabu. I know how it looks, but—'

'But what?' Prabu asked. 'Since we met, you only want to make the fun of me.'

'That's not true. You know I've been good to you.'

'I know you look down upon me. You think I am the inferior.'

'The last thing anyone can call me is a racist,' Indika said.

'I have not said you are racist. I say you look down to me thinking I am a stupid, because I do not know so much the ways of behave in a city. Because I am junglie villager. My English isn't so good. But you know what? I can speak my own language of Tamil. Everyone think you are smart, but how much of your own language can you speak?'

'Very little, I admit.'

'And everything you do is from the Western ways. How can I know how to behave like Western? How? You think I am a stupid?'

'You're smarter than me in so many ways.'

Prabu faked a laugh. 'I wish you knew how you sound, brother. I am not smart. I know that.'

'You play cricket like a genius,' Indika said. 'And you're like a brother—'

Prabu waved an arm and shook his head. 'Everything else I can make forgive. But you know I love the Achala. You know I really love her, not just like a joke for you with girls. This my only chance for a girlfriend.'

'I know, machan, but she's not good enough for you.'

'That is for me to make decide, no? You cannot make that decide and then—'

'It wasn't planned, I swear.'

Prabu watched waiters lighting half-shells of coconuts doused in kerosene to illuminate the pool veranda.

'How you felt when you believed I snog Isabella? How you feel? You make me get a beating and I not even do it.'

'But you told me you did,' Indika said.

'And how you feel?'

'I wanted to die.'

'And I was stranger to you then. I lose Achala and I lose my brother.'

'I know. I can imagine how it felt.'

Prabu put his hand around Indika's neck. 'It still feel. It still feel.' He let go as the murmurs of the Europeans got louder. 'I learn you have no value for our friendship and I learn Achala only stay with me to get to you.'

'She's screwed up.' Indika raised his hand. 'But that's for you to judge.'

'I never know how you can do that to me,' Prabu said. 'I never know.' He fell forward on to Indika's shoulder. Started crying. He couldn't control it. A tsunami of tears, down his face and through the debris of his moustache. 'Why'd you do it, brother?'

Indika's tears dripped between Prabu's bare toes. 'The thought of losing you as a friend destroys me. You're probably the only person I've ever got close to. You've seen the real me.'

'And I don't like it.'

Indika laughed. 'Well, that's fair enough. But please, I can't lose you.'

'You know as well as I know I have not a hope in the hell to pass my exams. I work like psychotic and nowhere close to understand my course. I fail, they kick me back into my camp.'

'We can study together. I'll never let them send you back there. I absolutely swear on my life.' Indika offered his hand to Prabu. 'Friends?'

Prabu knew that even if he could forgive he would never be able to forget. How could he ever trust Indika again?

'You never make a snog with Achala again?' Prabu asked.

'I can barely look her in the eye. She knows I lied about God, and now she thinks I'm the devil.'

'My father always he say that we must forgive for the war to end.'

'I completely agree.'

Prabu watched a tropical storm approaching over the Indian Ocean. He put a hand on either of Indika's shoulders, looked at his feet and said, 'But I can never forgive you for this.'

Patting Indika on the head, Prabu turned away from the storm and ran for cover. He didn't want to look back, but he did. Elephants, Kandyan dancers and drenched guests scurried under the marquee on the beach.

Indika slumped into a chair. Even though the rain thrashed against his face, his mouth remained open, eyes scrunched up.

He looked like someone howling in a silent movie.

THIRTY-ONE

Prabu didn't reply to any of Indika's messages.

He thought about it because he desperately needed some help studying.

But he had morals.

As things stood, Prabu didn't have a clue about basic geography, economics or history.

He didn't seem to have much of a clue about basic friendship either.

The rain crashed through the cracked windows of Prabu's boarding house, flooding the floor of his dormitory. His geography notes slipped off his new plastic sheets and into the water. He could use this as an excuse, surely, but like his father said, minorities should never make excuses. They should make strides.

The other boarders tried to help; even those who had subjected him to torture when he first arrived.

Yet nothing could match Indika's invitation to study at his house, under solid shelter, with dry books, hot food and clean sheets. Indika even had a tutor staying the night to help him prepare.

Prabu had never cared much for exams. The other Tamils at Mother Nelson Mahatma worked hard, dominating the top positions in each class. Prabu had a sense of letting them down. But what did it really matter? Life wasn't all a competition. For him it was survival. If he failed the exams, he would be sent back to the camp before he had a chance to complete the mission. The special mission for his people.

So he had to pass.

But pass, as unlikely as that sounded, and he'd still be Coach Silva's slave.

Prabu prepared himself to deal with that threat if it arose. For now, his focus had to be on kicking the butt out of these exams, but it felt like he had to do so without any shoes; hell, it almost felt like he didn't even have legs.

He lay back on his mattress, balancing his books on his stomach to keep them dry. Using *Economics Explained* as a pillow, he turned to the first page of his history notes.

The name Joseph Stalin rang a bell.

Adolf Hitler? Churchill? No Sri Lankan names.

Tikiri had dropped off a file of summarized notes, which reeked of the coconut oil from her hair. She had broken history down into fourteen pages, each page the answer to a possible essay question.

Poor old Tikiri bore the brunt of most of Indika's classroom jokes, but she was a genius who had a much better chance than the Papadum King of getting into Oxbridge.

She also dropped off a practice economics multiple-choice paper. Prabu remembered the sample answer that the teacher had given in class. He couldn't remember the question but the answer was definitely 'D'. One paper he could pass at least. He chose 'D' as the answer for all thirty-five questions and then took out the answer key to self-mark.

Baffled, Prabu noticed that A, B and C also showed up as answers to numerous questions and he ended up scoring 23 per cent.

A rat scurried past him, brushing his arm and making him jump, tipping the mattress over and dunking all his notes and books into an inch of water. The boy on the mattress next to him helped him to rescue the study sheets, but it was too late.

Lying back down, his hair stuck to the wet plastic, Prabu looked up at the fan as it stuttered around. His eyes glazed over a little, and it felt like the fan stayed still and the room spun around it.

He jumped back on to his feet, splashing the boy next to him. He reached for the first shirt he could see, which happened to be the pink Ralph Lauren Indika had lent him, made famous by the YouTube clip from the Wok. It reminded him of his first date with Achala. Good memories turned to puke. As always.

Slipping on his flip-flops, he climbed the stairs up to the water tank, where he had hidden his stash of cigarettes and magazines with pictures of topless women. He found his backpack. The backpack.

He ran down the stairs and out on to the street. The rain lashed across his face as he sprinted against the direction of the wind. His head felt like it would explode. He ran up Jawatte road, turning right on to Bullers Road. He passed the Bandaranaike Memorial International Conference Hall and the cathedral, and turned right at the British High Commission. He put his head down and charged towards the metal fencing around his school.

He remembered Suddha the monkey, and how he would climb into the school from the roof, under the satellite dish. This was Prabu's moment. He had a mission, and if he failed his exams, that would be destroyed. So he had to take decisive action now.

He had no other choice. He had been backed into a corner by those with power, and he needed to stand up for himself. Simply no other way he could think of. He had to break into school.

THIRTY-TWO

The shooting stops. The shelling never does.

I see you under a tree, rubbing the saltwater off your wounds. Licking the cut on your wrist. And you're watching your father. He's shoving something down the barrel of his gun. He's wiping sweat off his forehead. He's ignoring you.

It's true the Supreme Leader is dead. One Panther repeats the speculation that he was shot while surrendering, but another Panther goes crazy when he hears this. Beats the shit out of the speculator.

'The Supreme Leader would never surrender alive.'

They all say the war will end soon.

The only person who is allowed to consider surrendering is you. Because you're the special one. The Jose Mourinho of the Panthers. You have a mission, and you will stop at nothing to get it done.

The Panthers talk about you openly. They call you Magnificent Seven and they say you are a good-enough cricketer to win the northern scholarship to Mother

Nelson Mahatma International College. The boy who lost his family. The boy stuck in the war. The boy who'll captain Sri Lanka.

And they all know the plan. They can see the fire in your eyes. They know you have the drive, the passion, the belief in the friggin' cause.

They know that you will break into the school one night and plant explosives, and they know that you will wait for a special event to blow those Sinhalese bastards up.

So that those stuck-up pigs know what it feels like to lose a child. To lose a thousand children.

Tarzan has vanished, so Machine Gun Kelly is the only man from your troop you are sure is still alive. He briefs the twenty-eight men as they break from digging pits. Your father listens, his head in his hands.

'We have sent in your application already. The head of mathematics is a Panther funder. He is quite positive you will get in, maybe in a year, if they don't catch you before. Longer if they do.'

'I'll not stop till I get in,' you say.

'Well, you need to get in before you're eighteen.'

'Okay,' you say. 'I'll stop trying when I'm eighteen then.'

The Panthers laugh. You surprise yourself with how relaxed you are, and you wonder how proud your father is of you.

'The Papadum Dance would be a good time to strike,' Machine Gun Kelly says. 'Lots of youth, not so many adults. We want the adults alive, so they know what the pain feels like.'

You're trying to sleep, and I can see you being woken up by your own snoring.

Appa shines the light of his phone screen on your face. Runs a hand through your hair. 'What the hell are you doing here?'

'I'm the special one.'

He shakes his head, salty sweat flicking into your mouth. 'But you shouldn't be. I signed up because they said they would leave you be if I did. Leave you, Amma and Akka be. Have they taken them too?'

You shrug your shoulders. 'I don't know.'

'Are they alive?'

Wiping your eyes, maybe of tears, maybe of sweat, you say, 'It's been two years.'

'Since you saw them?'

You can't answer. Can't speak.

Appa digs a hand into his pocket. Pulls out a white flag. 'If anyone sees this, we're both dead.'

'What is it?'

'You know what it is.' Appa pulls you up to his chest. Hugs you so tight you can't breathe. 'You know what it is.'

'I'm not to surrender unless there is no other option,' you say. 'It's a last resort.'

'You will surrender tonight, my boy.' He kisses your head and it hurts because now he is crying and holding too tight.

'Is this the order from above?'

'This is the order from me, boy. Your bloody father.'

'But the mission—'

'All we hear about is the Magnificent Seven. A chosen boy, a special one. The boy who will get revenge for us. Bomb a school, show them how it feels.'

'Are you proud?'

He leans back out of the hug and slaps you. Three times. Forehand, backhand, forehand.

'Appa,' you say.

He grabs you by your collar and shakes you. 'What kind of an animal have you become?'

You are confused. What has happened to your father? 'Appa, why, why?'

'Even before I knew it was you, I was disgusted. Disgusted that we are trying to kill innocent children.' Now your father is holding his breath. 'Even before I knew it was my own blood, my own child, my one son. A friggin' mass murderer.'

You're getting angry. You want to slap your father back. He's an idiot. 'They're the murderers. Cowards and murderers.'

He slaps you before you have the chance to catch his arm. He shows you his hands. 'I have blood on these. Sinhalese blood. Two young boys. Maybe eighteen. You in three years. I killed them because they were army. Sent to fight.'

'But they would have killed you—'

'No one even knows what they're fighting for any more. No one knows. It's just blind bloody hatred.'

'I know why I'm fighting,' you say. 'I know why I will kill those Sinhalese bastard children.'

'No, you don't,' Appa says. 'You think you do, but you don't.' He lifts a finger to his lips, pushes your head against the ground and ducks down too so you both evade the spotlight. The one Machine Gun Kelly operates.

You know you have to be silent. You hate your father at this very moment, but you don't want to get him killed. Because really you love him even if he has gone crazy. And the spotlight hovers above you, so you have to be quiet for ten minutes. Maybe more. And so, finger in your mouth, sucking it, you think. Why is Appa like this? What has happened to him?

For those ten minutes, he doesn't release the grip on your shirt. If anything, it gets tighter.

Then, a whisper. 'The army didn't kill those girls.'

You are too confused to even hear him.

'They didn't kill Tanaja,' Appa says. 'They didn't kill her sister.'

You tug his grip off your shirt, ripping it. 'I saw them, Appa. I bloody saw them.'

'You saw them dead, but the army didn't kill them. Machine Gun Kelly killed them. At the Supreme Leader's order.'

THIRTY-THREE

Squatting near the main gate, Prabu planned to wait till the security guard went on a round before he climbed over. He hid for over fifteen minutes. One of the guards came out to switch off the light outside his security hut.

The guard wrapped himself in a blanket. Blowing into his hands, he looked up, and the raindrops crashed into his open eyes, forcing him back into his hut.

Prabu took off Indika's pink shirt and wrapped it around a coconut tree, pulling at it as he pressed his feet flat against the trunk. His backpack on his bare skin, he established a firm grip on the tree.

It took four heaves to get high enough to be able to stand on the top of the metal fence, with each of his feet wedged between sharpened metal spikes.

Throwing the pink shirt over first, he leapt down into the school grounds and ran to the back of the building. A square block, with barred windows lit up by floodlights, it resembled a prison even more at night than it did during the day.

Prabu crouched his way up the external fire escape.

By the time he reached the second floor, the storm had passed and bats jostled from tree to tree. Squeezing the excess water out of his shirt, he left it hanging off the fire escape handrail to dry.

The breeze disappeared, and as the humidity rose, Prabu felt warm sweat dripping down his temples. The change in weather allowed the three guards to come out on to the basketball court. Each undid the buttons of his shirt before one of them lit a cigarette and passed it around.

Prabu made it up to the roof and searched out the satellite dish. An inch or two of water had gathered on the flat ground around it, making it difficult for him to find the hatch opening into the building. Once he did, he encountered another problem. If he lifted the hatch, the water would pour down into the fourth floor corridor.

He couldn't leave a trail. Shouldn't.

After a moment's thought, he opened the hatch and watched the water drain in, hoping the school authorities would blame Suddha the monkey for the mess.

Lying flat on his belly, Prabu stuck his head through the hatch, but couldn't see anything and wished he had brought a torch.

He heard a musical car horn at the gate, which went on for at least thirty seconds. Running to the edge of the roof, he looked down and saw Coach Silva getting out of a white van, slapping a security guard across the back of the head. He locked his van and grabbed a bunch of keys from the guard's hut.

Running back to the hatch, Prabu squeezed through.

He dropped down, his feet skating ahead of him so he landed on his backside.

He knew the risks involved, but he had to switch on a light. He looked up at the hatch, wondering how Suddha got back up there to get out. It seemed too high to reach by jumping up and gripping, and anyway, he needed to be able to push the hatch open first.

How did Suddha do it?

Prabu realized how.

Suddha was a monkey.

Prabu's phone beeped. He put it on silent and then read the message.

From Indika: 'Whether you like it or not, I'm coming to help you study for your exam. There in five.'

He put his phone back in a plastic pouch, which he shoved into his damp pocket.

He needed an alternative plan. He could pull a desk out from one of the classrooms, but then it would be obvious to the school authorities that someone had broken in, and he couldn't do anything that would jeopardize the Papadum Dance.

He switched the light off when he heard Coach Silva shouting filth at a security guard a couple of floors below. He had to act quickly. He would deal with how to get out later.

Creeping down the main stairs, he passed the third floor, trying to work out where Coach Silva had gone. The second floor lights were all on. Prabu heard music from the conference room television just as a security guard walked in with a bottle of arrack and a rice packet.

The guard exited the room, looking back several
times to catch another glimpse of whatever Coach Silva
was watching. After the guard went back down the
stairs, Prabu sucked in a deep breath. He took off his
flip-flops and crept along the corridor to the entrance of
the conference room. Coach Silva sat on a leather chair
at the head of the table, Fashion TV's late night nudity
projected on the wall in front of him. He appeared to be
naked, but on closer inspection Prabu saw that he wore
tiny Y-front underpants, which were almost hidden by
flaps of fat. Sipping arrack straight from the bottle, he
mixed the contents of the rice packet with his left hand.

Having captured just over a minute of footage on his
phone, Prabu ran back to the stairs. He switched on a
light as he got to the third floor, and there in front of him
… exactly what he needed.

The exam paper cabinet.

He needed papers for three subjects. Or he'd fail.
A failure, returning home, cap in hand. Tail between his
legs.

He realized that he had to be very quiet now that Coach
Silva had decided to show up. Grabbing the handle of the
cabinet, he yanked it down quickly, as if pulling the flush
on an ageing toilet.

First time, it didn't budge.

He pushed the door and then tried again, yanking
harder.

No joy.

He balanced on the handle of the cabinet door. Then,
climbing on to the table on which the photocopier lay,

he stood on the handle, bouncing up and down, until it clicked loudly and broke off. The door swung open, knocking Prabu on to the floor with a thud.

He lay on his back, biting his right fist. His left leg had gone numb. The music from the conference room stopped. Footsteps and the sound of dragging feet. Prabu had to get out of there. But first, the papers.

Each of the eight shelves had a stack of bulging brown envelopes. Prabu pulled down one pile, discovering them all to be Grade Six exam papers. He placed them back, not quite as he had found them. He tried another shelf. Grade Nine papers. On the third attempt, he found the Grade Eleven papers, but there were about forty envelopes.

'Security,' Coach Silva called out. 'Security, you lazy shits.'

Prabu let all the envelopes drop to the floor, spreading them out like a pack of cards. He created a new pile of envelopes for physics, mathematics, biology, chemistry and English literature exam papers.

'Why the hell is the light on upstairs?' Coach Silva asked. 'You want to advertise to the whole world that I am here?'

'Sir, I didn't on the light. Maybe sometimes Suddha the monkey?'

'You're the bloody monkey. Switch off the bloody light.'

Prabu had located the economics paper, but still had to find the ones for history and geography. He heard the security guard's flip-flops slapping against the stairs. He threw all the envelopes back in, bar the exam papers he needed. Slammed the door shut. It made more noise than he thought it would.

'Suddha?' a security guard said, his footsteps slowing down.

'What the hell's happening up there?' Coach Silva asked.

'I think it is Suddha,' the guard replied. 'Sometimes monkeys can be too much strong.'

Prabu scurried into a classroom. Closed the door. He looked through the keyhole and saw the handle of the cabinet hanging off the door. Even a sleepy guard should notice that. On his hands and knees, he rushed out like a toddler on speed.

'You stupid chicken get your asshole upstairs and check if it's only the monkey,' Coach Silva said.

The footsteps began again. Prabu put his feet up against the cabinet, leaned back and tore off the handle.

Back in the classroom, he watched the guard shining a torch on the cabinet even though the lights were on.

'Hello, monkey?' the guard said. 'I give banana if you come.' He made kissing noises. 'Good monkey want banana?' Squatting down, he hooked his finger through the gap where the handle should have been and opened the cabinet door.

Rising back to his feet, he leapt down the stairs, saying, 'Coach Silva, Coach Silva, I think someone is break in.'

Prabu exited the classroom.

He heard a slap and the guard squealing.

'You stupid bloody shit,' Coach Silva said. 'How did someone get in?'

'Please, sir, let go my testes. They are paining.'

'Are they still in the building?'

'My testes?'

'No, you jackasshole.' Another slap. 'The bloody rogues.'

'Sir, I think sometimes it may be students. They ran a sack in the exam papers cabinet.'

Coach Silva roared. 'I want to kill you. Get the other guards and tell them to catch the bastards who are in here.'

Prabu had come this far. The school would know someone had broken in. He pulled out the papers he needed and placed the envelopes back in the cabinet. He realized that the school could create a shortlist of suspects based on which papers had been taken.

He tore open envelopes for other subjects and classes, shoving random papers into his backpack.

Footsteps from the ground floor. More security guards, three in all, now edged their way up the stairs to the third floor.

Prabu pushed the cabinet over. The screeching of metal on concrete sounded like gunfire. Bringing up bad memories. Being shot at. Diving into water.

He heard the guards running back down the stairs.

'You chicken shitty panties,' Coach Silva said. 'I'll go up.'

Prabu ran up the stairs to the fourth floor, away from Coach Silva's heavy breathing.

Pulling out a desk from a classroom, Prabu clambered on to it and tapped at the hatch, but he couldn't get it open.

The footsteps got louder.

Prabu jumped down, put a chair on the table and climbed back on top of it. He hit at the hatch with the heels of his palms. It clicked open and water cascaded through, drenching him.

He stuck his head through the hatch.

'I can see you, you bastard,' Coach Silva said.

Prabu struggled to pull himself up as his arms got in the way of his shoulders.

'I'm here, sir,' a guard said.

'Grab the monkey's legs,' Coach Silva said.

'That not monkey, sir,' the guard said. 'That is human legs.'

'I know, idiot boy. Grab them.'

Prabu had his shoulders above the hatch when he felt someone tugging at his feet. He kicked down and heard the clatter of chair on cement.

He shut the hatch behind him and sat on it while he caught his breath. He could hear and feel someone punching at it from below.

One, two, three. Prabu stood up, and the hatch flew open.

He sprinted for the fire escape, skidding as he put the brakes on near the edge of the building. He fell into a press-up position, his backpack slipping out of his grip. The brown envelopes, the exam papers, landing on the courtyard below.

He rocked back into a squat and looked down. Jumping off, he landed badly on the fire escape a floor below. He tried to stand, but his knee could barely support his weight. He limped down another flight of stairs. Two of the guards were one floor above him and closing in.

He wanted to grab the pink shirt he had left to dry on the second floor, but time ran out and he jumped over the handrail, straight on to the cemented pavement below.

He tried to stand, but his ankle gave way, so he lay flat on his stomach, just out of the beam of the third guard's flashlight.

Picking up a rock, Prabu hurled it at a window on the other side of the courtyard. The sound of smashing glass drew the guard's attention, and Prabu rolled behind Coach Silva's white van. He crawled towards the envelopes, scooping up the economics and history papers, but geography remained out of his reach.

The guards on the fire escape limped down and handed the pink shirt to Coach Silva as he came through the main door.

He raised the shirt up to his face and sniffed it.

The rain lashed down, forcing the guards back into their hut.

Prabu grimaced as he pulled himself up using the open window of Coach Silva's white van. He climbed on to the roof of it, and with one deep breath and a short prayer, leapt over the spiked fence.

His right foot slipped from under him as he did so, which turned his jump into more of a dive. This helped him clear the fence, but he landed badly on his left arm. He rolled into the deep gutter on the side of the road and ducked under water. It felt familiar being underwater, but he didn't know why. Lying on his back so only his nose, mouth and eyes remained above water, he tried to breathe even though golf-ball-sized raindrops spat against his face.

Coach Silva drove his van, at no more than ten miles per hour, up and down the road with his headlights on full beam. After five laps, he returned to the guard hut and chucked the pink shirt at the guards. 'Report this to Principal Uncle and give him this shirt. Remember, I wasn't here.'

He rolled up his window and sped off.

The guards wrapped themselves up in their blankets and closed the door to their hut.

THIRTY-FOUR

You don't want to believe your father. You don't want to believe that you have been manipulated like this. Worst, you don't want to believe that Tanaja and Raaga were killed because of you. Because the Supreme Leader wanted you for his mission. Wanted you to be angry. To be passionate. Wanted you to kill.

'Two little girls,' Appa says. 'Beauties, I hear. Torn from their families. Used as bait. Murdered to make you an assassin.'

'How do you know this?' You can't show him you're crying.

'Machine Gun Kelly's been bragging. Says once you complete your mission, he should be a martyr too. Without him, he says, you'd never kill.'

You open and close your mouth. Open and close. A question you want to ask, but you don't want the answer.

'You want to know how he did it?' Appa asks.

You wobble your head, tears landing on your knees.

'Claims he knew they were trying to escape, so he punished them. Drove them far away from camp. Left them there for an hour. Told them to run, then hunted them. Shot the younger one first in front of the elder one.'

You clench everything, not just your fists. Even your toes.

'You can't kill him,' Appa says. 'You have to get away.'

You look into the spotlight. Straight at Machine Gun Kelly, but you are blinded.

'He'll meet our maker,' Appa says. 'He'll pay.'

But this is not good enough for you. The evil prick wanted you to be a killer and now you are one, and there's just one person you want to kill.

Appa grabs your biceps. Shakes you. 'Snap out of it.'

You want to snap Machine Gun Kelly's neck. 'Does the Supreme Leader have any living relatives?'

'This is why there's a war,' Appa says. 'It's always going to be an eye for a bloody eye, and soon we will all be bumping into each other.'

'I need to, Appa, please understand.'

He slaps you again, and now your cheek is tender. 'You do as your father says. You remember this, okay, you're a kid. You can't be blamed for anything. You can still have a life.'

'Appa, what are you saying?'

'You surrender. You learn the ways of peace.'

'But my mission—'

Whack. 'What bloody mission? You want to murder kids?'

You pull at your own hair, and now you're crying loud enough to wake those around you.

'Stupid bloody kid.' Appa gets to his feet. 'Doesn't remember my ground rules.' He ambles over to Machine Gun Kelly. 'What the hell have you done to this boy?'

'Trained him to be the special one. The Magnificent Seven.'

'Well you've made him too cocky. No respect for his elders.'

You're digging a pit for your elders. For them to bunker in when the army makes its final push. Your father brings you some water.

You drop to your knees and kiss his feet. 'Sorry, Appa.'

'You know what you must do?'

'I know,' you say.

'What is your mission?'

'To survive.'

Your father's plans are methodical. He draws maps and shit. Shows you where to break away from the Panthers. Shows you how to get off the peninsula. Shows you where to surrender.

'You need bare land,' he says. 'So you don't surprise them. Strip down to your pants, so they know you're not packing. White flag above your head, stretched out, like a bloody sail. Don't mess that up.'

'What about you?'

'I'm a man. A grown bloody man. I'm responsible for my actions. No army bugger's going to take pity on a scumbag like me.'

You understand, but still. It's not good enough for you. You can't leave your father to die on the peninsula. 'Come with—'

'No.' He shakes his head, sweat flying off his moustache in patterns. 'No, no, no. They'll shoot at me, and you may die.'

You take out your white flag.

'Put that away, you idiot.'

You jump into the pit you dug so no one can see. Spreading the white flag out to its full length, you tear off half. 'Keep this, Appa.'

Your father jumps into the pit. Takes his half of the white flag. Puts it in his pocket and hugs the breath out of your lungs. You can feel his tears on your shoulder.

You know the map by heart. So as the moon hides behind a cloud, you tiptoe, crouching, out of the camp. But you stop. You want to see your father again. He must know that because he comes to you. Kisses you on the head. 'I love you, son.'

'When will I see you?'

'Find your amma and akka first. Give me a year. I'll find you.'

But stories are already filtering into the camp about soldiers shooting at men with white flags. You know this is the last time you will ever see your father. You know there is an even chance you may be killed, but a much greater likelihood that he will be.

'Don't cry,' Appa says. 'Just make us proud.'

'Appa, please—'

'Shhhh.' He holds the back of your neck. He bites his own wrist to stifle his sobbing. 'Now go.'

THIRTY-FIVE

Prabu hobbled past the day shift security guards at the school gates. The usual noises of his peers playing cricket or practising for the Papadum had faded into exam silence. Something about the lack of noise made him sweat more than usual.

He shivered despite the sun beating down. With every step, he expected someone to grab his arm and drag him up to Principal Uncle's office, but nothing happened.

Rocking back and forth in his chair in the exam hall as he waited for his economics multiple-choice paper, Prabu instinctively acknowledged Indika's wave, but then turned away before he may have had to smile.

The examiner placed Prabu's question paper face-down on his desk.

'Turn the papers over and start writing. You have one hour.'

Prabu recognized the first question and the second and the third. The whole damn paper, exactly like the one he had stolen. An exact copy of the Advanced Level unit 1 paper from January 2008, for which Prabu had all the answers. ABDCADBC: the answer key written on his right ankle, which he now had crossed over his left thigh.

The explanations, one mark for each of four points made. Prabu had them all written on the inside of his shirt. Just had to ensure that he didn't finish too early.

He scratched his head, grunted, bit his pencil and frowned; all for the benefit of the examiner. Then he realized if he got too many answers right, the teachers would get suspicious; for three random questions he changed the answer and crossed out his explanation.

Time up.

Leaning back in his chair, Prabu closed his eyes. Something wasn't right.

Limping to the door, Prabu watched the examiner rub the exam times off the whiteboard, replacing them with the hours of the next exam. Prabu flicked through the stack of exam papers, pulled his out and dropped it in his bag.

He shuffled into the corridor.

Tikiri found him as the school bell sounded, ringing continuously for thirty seconds.

'Fire alarm?' Prabu asked.

'Special assembly, apparently,' she said.

'Oh.' Prabu stopped breathing.

'You're going red. Well, purple, really. Dark purple.'

He had to be strong here or the game would be over.

'What's wrong?' Tikiri blushed. 'You look terrified. Something you want to ask me?'

Deep breath. Think. Think. What does she mean? 'Yes, but scared to ask.'

'I'll say yes, so go ahead.'

'You won't slap me again?'

Tikiri giggled, waggled her thick eyebrows. 'No, of course not.'

'If you're not here only to study, will you come to the Papadum with me? As my date?'

Tikiri made whimpering noises, much like Prabu used to make when Achala talked to him. 'With the future Papadum King? How could I say no?' She grabbed Prabu's hand and swung his arm up and down all the way to assembly.

Principal Uncle stood at the assembly lectern, hands on hips. He shook his head at each and every student who caught his eye.

Prabu thought seriously about running, but knew his knee wouldn't hold up.

Principal Uncle said, 'Silence. Silence.'

The students chattered as they took their seats.

Principal Uncle leaned into the microphone. 'I am about to cancel the Papadum unless I get your full cooperation.'

Everyone sat down. Stopped talking.

'After a marvellous term, we have come up against the worst disciplinary problem we have ever had at this school.' He paused to sip water, bending down to pick up a plastic bag out of which he pulled the pink shirt Prabu had left at school the night before.

Tikiri turned to Prabu and whispered, 'Isn't that yours?' as soon as she saw it. 'The one you were wearing in that YouTube clip?'

Prabu raised his finger to his lips. Mimicked a knife

slashing his neck. Turning to his right, he saw Indika staring straight at him, mouthing, 'Is that mine?'

Prabu shook his head. Looked down.

Principal Uncle said, 'Someone left this shirt on the fire escape last night.'

A few pupils snickered.

'The boy who left it broke into the school like a petty thief and ransacked the exam paper cabinet.'

Loud murmuring.

'Shut up. Now listen, children, and I call you children when I should be calling you babies. The integrity of the exam process has been compromised and the exams will be called off for this term.'

The murmuring increased in volume. The six founding members of the Scorpion Five shared their gang handshake.

'I wouldn't smile if I were you,' Principal Uncle said. 'Since we can't hold the exams this week, because the teachers need time to set new papers, we will have to hold them next week. I have no choice but to cancel the Papadum.'

Silence.

'And that's not it. Once you have finished those exams, we will make you sit another set over the holidays. So your hero or heroes who broke in have cost you the Papadum and your holidays. Anyone smiling now?' Principal Uncle looked around and downed the glass of water. 'I didn't think so.'

He turned off the microphone, made as if to walk away from the lectern. He stopped, put his finger to his chin and said, 'Oh yes.' Returning to the microphone, he said, 'I've just had a thought. Maybe if the animal who stole the papers owns up, we can go ahead as normal.' He lifted the pink shirt up again. 'Can the owner of this shirt please stand up?'

Principal Uncle looked around, as did Prabu and everyone else.

'Let me reiterate the gravity of this situation. Some of you are never allowed out at night except for school events. If you miss out on the Papadum, which I must add will never be held again, then maybe you miss out on a social life. But that's not important. What is important is that some of you need your end-of-term exam grades for your US university applications. Maybe some of you are not applying this year? Well, do you want your holidays cancelled?'

Silence.

'All it takes is for someone to stand up and tell me whose shirt this is.'

Heads swayed from side to side like a crowd at a tennis match.

Prabu couldn't be sure if he was imagining this, but it sounded like people were whispering his name, along with the words 'YouTube' and 'the Wok'.

He knew everyone had seen that clip a number of times. Thanks to YouTube, he had been accepted faster than he could have ever hoped, but now it could end up being the cause of his rejection.

Prabu looked down at his feet. Time to own up. Maybe he could plead his case not to be sent back to camp.

He sat up, pressed his feet against the ground and tried to stand up, but his ankle and knee couldn't hold his weight. He tried again, but gave up as soon as he heard the murmuring.

Achala was on her feet, to his right, her hand in the air. 'I know whose shirt that is.'

THIRTY-SIX

No one spoke in the assembly hall.

Prabu noticed Indika trying to make eye contact with him again, but he locked his own gaze on the stage, where Coach Silva sat with four teachers.

Whispers turned into murmurs, turned into clear speech.

Achala had returned from the principal's office.

She approached Prabu, put a hand under his chin and kissed him on the lips. Smiled at Tikiri. 'Your lips taste as sweet as revenge.'

She stood tall and called out, 'Indika. Daddy made me tell the truth about whose shirt that is. Principal Uncle's waiting for you in his office.' Running a hand through Prabu's hair, she said, 'That will teach him to spurn me.'

Indika smiled, waved to all the other students and said, 'Don't worry. It wasn't me. See you in ten.'

Prabu ran out of the assembly hall, skidding across the mud on the basketball court. He bent over near the mango tree. Started retching, but nothing would come out.

'Everything okay?' Tikiri asked, out of breath, having run after him.

Prabu sat on the concrete bench under the tree. 'I do something very bad.'

Tikiri flicked both of her coconut-oiled plaits behind her shoulders and nestled her head against Prabu. 'I don't care what you've done.'

'I need to close both my eyes, please.'

Tikiri pushed his head down on to her lap and curled his hair around her fingers. They stayed like that for at least half an hour.

Coach Silva clutched a handful of Prabu's hair, pulling him up. 'You in shit so deep you need a jeep, boy. Principal Uncle wants to see you immediately.'

Prabu rose to his feet. Smiled at Tikiri, then turned and slouched away. He took a detour and found Gajen stuffing his face with seeni sambol buns.

'You have Shock Ice's number?'

Gajen nodded, his mouth too full to speak.

'Text to me, okay? Please. It is urgent. He is still stalking that hairy girl Leah?'

Finishing off chewing, Gajen said, 'Not just stalking, dude. Genuinely dating.'

'That is good. Please to send now because Principal Uncle, he is waiting for me.'

Crossing the basketball court, Prabu stopped to copy and paste Shock Ice's number into a new message, which read: 'Because I have much of respect for you and your family, I have to tell to you that Indika Jayanetti has make a bet that he will snog Leah at our school's Papadum Dance.'

Relying on the banister, Prabu dragged himself up to the first floor landing.

Indika exited Principal Uncle's office, approaching Prabu, head bowed. Grabbed his hands. 'Just remember, whatever happens, you're always my brother.'

Prabu pulled his hands out of Indika's grip. 'Please, just go.'

Indika forced his arms around Prabu and gripped him tight enough to show anyone watching that they were friends. 'I guess I'll never see you again, so goodbye, machan. It's been an adventure.'

That was it. That was too much. Patronization gone too far. Prabu forced his arms out by his side, breaking Indika's grip on him. 'Screw off, you evil bastard. I hate you. I hate you. I hate you.'

He marched away, the pain in his knee no longer bothering him.

'Wait,' Indika called out.

Prabu froze but didn't turn around.

'Goodbye, my brother,' Indika said.

Prabu imagined him laughing, mocking, smirking, taking the piss.

Once too often, he thought.

His phone pinged. A text message from Shock Ice, which read, 'He's dead.'

THIRTY-SEVEN

Prabu entered Principal Uncle's office without even knocking.

'Everything Indika tell to you is true,' he said. 'I not make a denial.'

'So you did try to stop him?' Principal Uncle asked.

'I beg for your pardon, sir.'

'Indika told us you tried to talk him out of it.'

'Out of admit it his shirt?'

Mr Carter said, 'Out of breaking into school.'

'I don't follow what you say, sir. I am break into the school.'

Principal Uncle stood. 'Indika told us you might say that.'

'We know the dynamic,' Mr Carter said. 'He's the bad guy on your shoulder. You take the blame for everything.'

'Sir, he is not on my should—'

'One second, Prabu, before you say any more.' Mr Carter leaned towards him. 'You do realize if you actually were to convince us it was you, you'd be sent back to the camp.'

'I get sent back anyway, no?' Prabu asked. 'If I fail? How to pass these bloody exams?'

'By Indika stealing the papers for you?' Principal Uncle said.

'But just to clarify,' Mr Carter said. 'You didn't ask him to steal them?'

'Who is steal what, sir?' Prabu was baffled. He wondered for a second if he was listening in the wrong language.

'And when Indika tried to give you the papers, you refused to take them?' Mr Carter asked.

Prabu realized now what was happening, and all he could think of was Shock Ice. He pointed to the door. 'Sir, can I put a chat with Indika?'

'He's gone, son,' Principal Uncle said. 'I doubt any of us will see him again.'

'You understand the implications of this?' Mr Carter asked. 'You should have told us before it happened. Told us of Indika's intentions.'

'But we do appreciate that you didn't want to rat your friend out,' Principal Uncle said.

'There is something noble, some might say, in what he did,' Mr Carter said. 'Essentially, he was worried that you weren't ready to face an exam. Said it was unfair.'

'We are not here to debate fairness,' Principal Uncle said. 'Whether he thinks he was justified in his reasons for helping Prabu is immaterial. He broke the law.'

Prabu had absolutely no idea what they were saying. 'Sir, what is happen to Indika?'

'While I respect him for owning up, I'm afraid we had to let him go. Precedents and all that.'

'You're expel him, sir?' Prabu asked.

'Asked him to leave,' Principal Uncle said. 'He won't have to declare that we expelled him on his university applications, and we can give him a reference based on his brilliant record up to Grade Ten. But there's no way he can stay at school.'

Prabu looked at Principal Uncle, raised a hand and said, 'Can I put a chat with you and Carter sir in the private?'

'We're in private now,' Principal Uncle said. 'You have an exam to sit, and you're not getting out of that.'

'I have no chance to make a pass, sir. I also did not submit my economics multi-choice paper. There is no point as I have no right answers. Better, I think, I go to speak with the Indika.'

'Prabu, you have to think carefully,' Mr Carter said. 'I don't want you going back to the camp. Just sit the paper, son, and we'll work it out after, okay?'

Prabu sat by the window, bouncing his foot up and down.

Mr Carter passed the papers around. 'Wait till I tell you to start.'

Prabu flipped the paper over. He didn't feel anything. He didn't fear failure as he knew it was inevitable.

Scorpion Gayan leaned forward in his chair and said, 'What the hell happened to Indika, dude?'

Prabu shook his head.

'Expelled?' Gayan asked.

Prabu nodded.

'You seen his Twitter update? Says he's dead.'

Prabu stood up so fast, he knocked his chair over. 'Sorry, Carter sir.' He bent down to pick up his chair. Whispered to Gayan, 'Where is he?'

'I texted him. He said he's waiting in the admin office while the staff clear out his locker and give him his certificates and whatever.'

'At school?'

'Prabu, sit down,' Mr Carter said. 'Turn your papers over now.'

Prabu did as told, pretending to read the first question, but instead he worked on his own problem. Would Indika have enough time to get home before Shock Ice chased him down and kicked his ass?

He looked up at Mr Carter and mouthed, 'Sorry, sir.' Dropping his pencil, he picked up his bag and ran out of the exam hall.

Just as he was about to jump down a flight of stairs, Coach Silva wobbled out of a classroom with a crooked smile on his face. He shoved Prabu in the direction of the staff toilets, smashing him against the wall and closing the door behind them both.

'I told you to disappear before.' Coach Silva bent over his rice-belly. Picked up his rubber slipper. 'I gave you the chance to save face. A screw up, but maybe not a disgrace like you've become now. I know you're the bugger who broke into the school, so now I can expose you for everything you are. Unless ...'

Coach Silva grabbed Prabu's ass.

Prabu felt a tear run down his face, but he rubbed it away. He had controlled himself all these months, but now he saw images of dead girls. Of dying soldiers. Of his father saying goodbye.

He pushed Coach Silva against a cubicle door. Coach Silva bounced off it and raised his slipper.

But Prabu caught Coach Silva's wrist and shook it until the slipper dropped out of his grip. Using the wall for support, he lifted himself up and lobbed the slipper into the urinal.

He had never felt stronger. Taking a deep breath, he puffed out his chest and slammed Coach Silva against the door. Closing his eyes, he reminded himself not to do anything crazy now, so he turned to the main door.

But Coach Silva charged at him. Prabu dodged him, pushed him against the sink and held his face up against the mirror. Released his grip. 'You're not worth my shit even.'

Coach Silva's gaze switched to a cockroach, which he tried to crush with his left foot, but Prabu kicked his leg away. The cockroach fled under the door back into the corridor.

Prabu held up his phone. 'I have record you conversing with me, when you make threatens to me.'

Coach Silva lunged for the phone, but Prabu kicked at his ankles, dropping him, with a loud thud, to the floor.

'I'll have you killed, you little shit.' Coach Silva brushed himself off. 'I'd kill your family too if they weren't already—'

Bam. Bam. Bam. The bridge of Prabu's open palm against Coach Silva's nose. Snapping it. Making him clutch at it, screaming without any noise.

Bam. A hammer blow to the top of his head. Bam. Bam. Bam.

Coach Silva in a heap. Legs to his chest. Howling. Prabu kicked him, full on the ribs. Cracks.

Visions of dead girls. The taste of shit in Prabu's mouth. Muddy water through his teeth. Blood.

No surrender this time. Kill him. Kill him. Kill him.

Steven Mathews touching Prabu. Coach Silva touching him.

Kill.

But Indika.

Prabu ran out of the bathroom, the screams of a dirty old bastard behind him.

THIRTY-EIGHT

Prabu sprinted across the basketball court, past the canteen and up the stairs to the administrative and accounts offices.

He shouted out Indika's name before he realized that he wasn't there. He put both his palms on the bursar's desk. 'Please, sir, emergency. Location of the Indika?'

'Why do you have blood—'

'Please, sir.' Prabu grabbed the administrator by his collar.

'He left five minutes ago. That way.'

Prabu pulled open the fire exit door and stood on the external stairs he had used the night before. Shielding his vision from the noon sun, he spotted Indika across the road, about to get into a trishaw.

Indika was busy bargaining with the trishaw driver, appearing oblivious to his name being called. Prabu leapt down the stairs and charged towards the gate. Mr Carter came out, tried to stop him, but Prabu sidestepped him and ran through an open drain. 'Indika.'

Indika's trishaw started moving. Prabu ran towards it, knowing that he had to catch it before it gathered speed.

A Defender jeep appeared from out of a dirt road and drove straight at the trishaw, braking metres away from it. The trishaw swerved away from the jeep, balancing on two of its three wheels before collapsing on its side.

Prabu legged it towards the spot, watching as Shock Ice got out of a blood-red Hummer behind the Defender jeep.

Prabu couldn't decide whether to help Indika out of the trishaw first or try to stop Shock Ice and explain to him what had happened.

The second option seemed the wiser one because there was no point in pulling Indika out just for him to get pistol-whipped by a bunch of thugs.

'Shock Ice, sir, wait,' Prabu said between large gulps of air. 'Please, sir, wait.'

Shock Ice turned square on to Prabu, spread his legs and reached a hand into the back of his jeans.

'Machan, machan,' Indika shouted, his head poking out of the open side of the overturned trishaw.

'I'll bloody kill him,' Shock Ice said.

And now, can you remember, you see Shock Ice's guards as Panthers? You see them as Mr Majestyk and Machine Gun Kelly and Murphy's Law. And you see Shock Ice as the Supreme Leader, with Tanaja's and Raaga's blood on his hands.

He doesn't stand a chance. You have Shock Ice by the throat. His short legs thrashing in the air. And his guards point their guns at you, but they know they can't shoot. And so they try to grab you, but you hit them off. Elbows, headbutts, and you drop Shock Ice to the ground. In your head, he's everything bad that has happened to you. Your arms thrash and the blood gets in your eyes. Between your teeth.

Then you wake up. You breathe. What the hell are you doing?

Now the guards jump you. Pound you. Mr Carter tries to stop them, but he gets beaten away, and so does Indika. But then the sirens.

'Get in the bloody jeep,' Shock Ice says to his group of thugs.

And your eyes close. Swelling.

Now remember this. You spend two nights in a detention centre until Colonel Thisara gets you out. Mr Carter and Thathi are with him.

Thathi has something from Indika for you. The Papadum King crown. You're proud, but think it's probably not the best thing to wear as you leave captivity.

They put you in front of specialists who tell you none of this is your fault. You have memories that are locked. Memories that come out when you're pushed.

Memories no kid should have.

It's not your fault.

But you're not ready for school, they tell you. More rehab. Give it time. Maybe kickback in a home with a family like Indika's.

They say they can keep you.

Because you're a good kid.

Because, Prabu, you are me.

I open my eyes.

Dr Ratnayake looks concerned. 'So it worked?'

'I think so,' I say.

'These are scary memories you have.'

'Very.'

'But now you must control them,' Dr Ratnayake says. 'Not be surprised by them.'

THIRTY-NINE

Akka emailed me, but I have not met her yet, and to this day, I am not sure if it was she who sent the email or someone else pulling a sick prank. I have tried to find her, but if it is Akka, it seems she wants to remain hidden. Her way of coping, I guess. This is her email, translated from Tamil.

The war ended, I was able to live a normal life. When you hit the news, no one knew of my connection to you, and that was good for me.

I know we can't blame you for what you became. But at the same time, you shouldn't blame Amma.

She took me to the doctor the day I was hit by shrapnel, and if she hadn't, there's a good chance I would have died. How could a mother let her daughter die?

When we left you, she did not think for one second that she wouldn't return for you. And she did. Four days later. But you had gone.

They told Amma that you had been taken to a Panther training camp, but you'd be back soon. Amma howled

257

and hammered with closed fists at the chest of the Panther who told her this until he beat her across the face.

She slept outside that camp for five days, waiting for you to come to the fence. But you never did. She refused to eat till they brought you to her, and you know how Amma loved food.

I had to cremate her alone.

She was the last family I thought I had.

Many years later, I saw you on the BBC being paraded as an innocent little boy being given a chance to shine in Colombo.

I work as a nurse in a Jaffna hospital, and I pointed at the screen and wanted to say that's my thambi. My darling little brother, who I thought was dead.

The reason why I didn't come forward is that I had adopted a new persona. I was Nurse Betty, that was how people knew me.

I didn't want to be known as a Panther's sister.

I'm sorry.

One day, I will find you and we can share a hug. A hug like we should have had the last time we were with each other.

If you have found Appa, please tell him I'll find him too.

Love, your darling Nurse Betty.

FORTY

Four years later

Indika and I formed an NGO called Sri Lanka Together. It's run by young people, for young people. To help kids grow up trusting each other. For Tamils to understand that not all Sinhalese want to kill them. For Sinhalese kids to know Tamils aren't terrorists. To make sure the youth of Sri Lanka aren't haters. To do justice to this great country.

Indika works and lives in the north, me in the south. This would have been unthinkable a few years earlier.

I have been looked after by the Jayanettis. Sent abroad to study with Indika. Provided with therapy, which is still ongoing, because I will never fully recover from my memories.

But now, with Indika, I am part of a movement and I have just been on a bus, travelling the country. Kids from Colombo schools, Buddhist schools, came with me to Jaffna.

And in Jaffna, some of the kids had never seen a

Sinhalese in person before they met Indika, unless they were in uniform.

We meet a guy who wants to become a doctor, but he has no money. He says before we set up the office in Jaffna, he hated all Sinhalese, but now he knows they're the same as us. Humans. With hearts. With faults.

I tell him if he works hard, I'll help him get funding to study medicine.

When we leave we see a six-foot-two Sinhalese hugging a five-foot-one Tamil. They're crying. They met two days ago, neither one able to speak the other's language, but they're sad to say goodbye.

And I know there is hope.

Sri Lanka is such a beautiful country. We have it all; the beaches, the history, the hills, the heritage, the food, the smiling faces, the hospitality – and now the peace. I am getting used to this. I think I can move on.

I arrange my first cricket net since the incident at school almost four years ago. Indika is meant to travel down from Jaffna to smack some balls around with me, but his phone is off, so I assume he has forgotten. Instead, I call up some old friends; Gish and Gayan (Sinhalese Buddhists), Khuzi (Muslim), Gajen (Tamil Hindu), and Shoban (mixed-race Christian). All different, but all very similar. All just young guys, enjoying life, enjoying peace.

My batting technique is still strong, so the boys encourage me to take up cricket professionally. I am not too old, I know it, but do I have the heart? Is it my calling? Can I use my experiences to make a difference, like one of the greatest cricketers of all time, Kumar Sangakkara? He said, 'I am Tamil, Sinhalese, Muslim and Burgher. I am a Buddhist, a Hindu, a follower of Islam and Christianity. I am today, and always, proudly Sri Lankan.'

I speak to Mr Carter about this. I speak to Tikiri and the Jayanettis, but the guy I need to ask is still out of reach, and I am worried.

So I try Indika's phone for the twenty-first time and, thank god, it rings.

'Hello,' says the voice of a man I thought was dead.

'Where's Indika?' I ask.

'He's a little tied up right now,' Tarzan says. 'But don't worry, you know you can trust me.'

ACKNOWLEDGEMENTS

Thank you to the people of Sri Lanka for supporting my books. Please forgive me for fictionalizing the war for the sake of the story. This is my home, the place I love, the country I will never leave (unless deported).

Thanks, Kanishka Gupta. An agent of extraordinary talent and devotion. A wonderful man, a brilliant mind, a great character.

Neelini Sarkar shaped my first book and this one. Never will I write anything without knocking on her door. An incredible woman, wise, kind, delightful.

I greatly admire and am inspired by Manasi Subramaniam, my HarperCollins India editor. Everything she says about the book makes me stand up and clap. A creative genius, she understands this novel far better than I do. I am absurdly privileged to be working with her.

Prior to publication, I didn't show *Panther* to anyone from my own life, yet I am grateful to my friends, especially Mahela and Christina Jayawardena, Gishanka de Silva, Robin Hiney, Kenneth McAlpine, Priyanga

Hettiarachchi, Sarrah Sammoon and Hafsa Uvais for their continued help and enthusiasm.

My wife's friends have also been pure gold. Natasha and Radhik Colombage, Amir Abdeen, Kavita and Prasan Fernando, Githanji Kaluperuma and Chamendra Wimalasena. (By the way, I have more friends than my wife does.)

The brilliant new people I have met in the process of being published, such as Amish Raj Mulmi, Sayoni Basu and Sudha Pillai.

The ridiculously amazing PR guru, Pia Hatch, for getting my name out there. Simply. The. Best.

Shehan Karunatilaka, author of one of my all time favourite books, Chinaman, for being so generous with his time and advice.

Mum: there is no greater example of a human being.

Tashi, Sonam, Anna and Jack, all too funny, all too kind.

Charlie, Nimal, Rohini and Bianca. In-laws with a cause.

Samantha and Tara, my wife and daughter. The wife = selfless, beautiful, loving, encouraging, just plain too-damn-good-to-be-true. The daughter = funny, caring, invariably kind and so slap-me-in-the-face-to-remind-me-how-lucky-I-am sweet. She says, 'I love you, daddy,' I melt. Sam and Tara, I present to you, for you, and with you, this book, the next book and every book. Some authors have millions, some have prizes, most have talent. I have you two. What more do I need?